Lunatic ... or prophet?

I THINK MY SISTER'S wedding was the last good time we had in our family. Mama behaved well. Pegg and I dressed her in a good dimity and a lace-trimmed cap. I don't know if she understood what was going on.

When Pegg and I put her to bed that night, she smiled at us. "The tea," she said.

"You want tea, Mama?" I asked.

"The water will run brown with it," she said. "And after that, it will run red, with blood of Patriots."

I shivered. "Yes, Mama," I said.

"Don't you ever wed, Anne." She gripped my hand. "Marriage is not a good state. A woman gives up all her property and rights and privileges."

I thought of Spencer Roane. He and his father had been invited to today's wedding. He'd sat next to me and talked to me about horses. "It's refreshing to meet a girl who can talk about more than bread pudding," he'd said.

Again I said, "Yes, Mama." I blew out the candle and left her there in the dark, with her visions of water turning brown from tea, and then red from blood.

OTHER NOVELS BY ANN RINALDI

Brooklyn Rose

The Staircase

The Coffin Quilt
The Feud between the Hatfields and the McCoys

Cast Two Shadows
The American Revolution in the South

An Acquaintance with Darkness

Hang a Thousand Trees with Ribbons
The Story of Phillis Wheatley

Keep Smiling Through

The Secret of Sarah Revere

Finishing Becca
A Story about Peggy Shippen and Benedict Arnold

The Fifth of March
A Story of the Boston Massacre

A Break with Charity
A Story about the Salem Witch Trials

A Ride into Morning
The Story of Tempe Wick

Ann Rinaldi

Or Give

Me Death

A NOVEL OF
PATRICK HENRY'S FAMILY

HARCOURT, INC.
Orlando Austin New York
San Diego London

For information about permission to reproduce selections from this book,
write to trade.permissions@hmhco.com or to Permissions, Houghton
Mifflin Harcourt Publishing Company, 3 Park Avenue, 19th Floor,
New York, New York, 10016.

www.hmhco.com

First Harcourt paperback edition 2004

The Library of Congress has cataloged the hardcover edition as follows:
Rinaldi, Ann.
Or give me death: a novel of Patrick Henry's family/Ann Rinaldi.
p. cm.—(Great Episodes)
Summary: With their father away most of the time advocating
independence for the American colonies, the children of
Patrick Henry try to raise themselves, manage the family plantation,
and care for their mentally ill mother.
1. Henry, Patrick, 1736–1799—Family—Juvenile fiction. [1. Henry,
Patrick, 1736–1799—Family—Fiction. 2. Family life—Virginia—
Fiction. 3. Mental illness—Fiction. 4. Virginia—History—Revolution,
1775–1783—Causes—Fiction. 5. United States—History—Revolution,
1775–1783—Causes—Fiction.] I. Title. II. Series.
PZ7.R459Or 2003
[Fic]—dc21 2002027477
ISBN 978-0-15-216687-8
ISBN 978-0-15-205076-4 pb

Text set in Stempel Garamond
Designed by Cathy Riggs

DOC 20 19 18 17 16 15
4500670447
Printed in the United States of America

For my daughter, Marcella,
and son-in-law, Scott

Or Give Me Death

1771

Patsy

Chapter One

I WAS THE FIRST ONE in the family to know when Mama started to go insane. Somewhere along the line, when Pa was away speechifying against all those laws and writs and resolutions, she took leave of her senses.

I didn't want to admit it at first. Mama's tired, I told myself. Too much time alone. But then one day she dipped baby Edward into the basin of water because he was fretful.

Dipping a baby in water is no reason to think somebody is addled. But Mama wasn't about to take him out.

Baby Edward was just two months old, and he'd been crying for hours already. Nothing Silvy or Pegg or any of the other Negro servants did would stop him.

"The water will becalm him," Mama said.

But she had that same look in her eyes that I'd seen the day I found her in the middle of the English garden trying to take all her clothes off, and talking about how

3

the sun was her only friend. I got her inside right quick. That was the day she found out Pa was leaving once more.

"The House of Burgesses again." She looked mournful sad. And after that day she just went all inside herself.

Edward stopped crying, sure enough, when she put him in that water. He near turned blue.

"Mama," I said, "Mama." But gently. Lest she get a purchase on him that I couldn't break. She paid me no mind.

So I pulled my little brother out of the water. He was choking by then, and I did what Pa had taught me and John to do in case one of the other little ones fell into New Found River. I set him down on the wood table and pushed his chest until he got his breath.

"I can't abide his crying anymore," Mama was saying. She just kept saying it, over and over, while I set about getting Edward breathing, and Pegg, our cook, started praying to Jesus then and there.

Soon the commotion brought Pegg's children, who were always underfoot, anyway. From Shadrack, the oldest at twelve, to Nancy, Pleasant, Jessee, Reuben, and even Letty, the two-year-old.

"Is the baby daid? Is the baby daid?" five-year-old Reuben kept asking.

"Get the children out!" I ordered.

Pegg shooed them out.

"Take Mama to the front parlor."

She led Mama away.

"And keep a still tongue in your head." I was stern but kind, the way Pa had taught me to be with the Negroes.

But Pa was away again. Likely riding through the countryside to stop and call at taverns, stores, and plantations to talk about the new evils sent to us by the king. While he did not know of the evil going on here at home under his own roof.

Nobody in the family did yet. Except MyJohn, my intended. My betrothed. So far I'd managed to keep it between me and MyJohn.

I wrapped Edward in dry clothing. He was making little wheezing sounds. I put him in his cradle and went from the detached kitchen to the main house. I ran in the back door, through the long hall, where there were bloodstains on the heart-pine floors because of a duel once fought here. I was careful not to step on the bloodstains. All of us children were convinced it was bad luck to step on them.

There was nobody in the front parlor. What had Pegg done with Mama? I stamped my foot on the wide floorboards.

All eight rooms and the great hall were empty.

I ran upstairs to the top floor from where you could see Carter's Mountain and the foothills around Charlottesville.

Nobody.

I ran back downstairs to the cellar. In the rear was the bricked-up dry well.

It wouldn't be the first time Pegg had put her in there. "Bring her around," she'd said, last time. "Freeze the devil inside her."

"There's no devil in my mother. And don't you ever do it again!" I'd shouted.

I heard Mama crying behind the old, thick wooden door.

The dry well was old, old as the house itself. Old as the devils that tormented my mother. Pegg was right about that, but I'd never admit it. It was deep, too. Twenty-five feet long. The food was stored there in terrible coldness.

I pounded on the door. "Mama!" I yelled. "It's me, Patsy. What are you doing in there?"

"Pegg put me here. She said I near killed Edward. And I must pay for my sins."

"Mama, you haven't killed Edward. I've got him breathing right, and he isn't crying anymore. I'll find the keys and let you out."

"I've got the keys."

"Then why don't you open the door, Mama?"

"Pegg said I must stay here an hour. And pray. You'll tell me when the hour is up, won't you?"

Pegg! How dare she order Mama about, the mistress of the place! I felt a stab of fear. "Pegg is wrong, Mama. She had no right to do this to you."

"She said she'd tell your pa when he comes home, if I don't stay here an hour."

I leaned my forehead against the rough, old, thick wood of the door. I must becalm myself. Tell Pa? How dare she? If it was anyone's place to tell Pa it was mine. I knew I should tell him. Maybe I should write to him now. What would happen if I told him?

What would happen if I didn't? Would Mama kill Edward some other time, when I wasn't around to protect him? Would she put a pillow over his face at night? What would I do then? Still keep her secret? Say he died in his sleep? Babies did sometimes. Dark, unexplainable things happened all the time in the outlands of Virginia.

Look what had happened to Charles Chiswell, who'd once owned this very house. His son John ran his friend through the heart with a sword at Ben Mosby's Tavern at Cumberland Court House. All over a card game. Got away with it, too. It's what Pa calls the corruption of the aristocracy.

Mama is aristocracy. She is descended from Alfred the Great. Also King Edward the First. She has fourteen barons in her family. Surely that's too many barons. One lady ancestor, Mary Shelton, was lady-in-waiting to Queen Elizabeth.

"Mama, please open the door. Please. I'm saying you can come out now. You are the mistress of the plantation. You don't have to mind Pegg. And I won't let her tell Pa."

From behind me then came a clattering of shoes down the wooden steps, voices like a flock of blue jays. My brothers and sisters, come to gawk.

"What's wrong, Patsy?" It was John, my brother, a year younger than I, a head taller. He'd be tall, like Pa, John would soon. The same blue eyes, too.

"Get the children out of here," I told him.

Beyond stood Will, eight; Anne, seven; and Betsy, two, all staring.

"Where's Mama?" Anne asked. She sensed things. I was convinced she had uncommon powers. She always did know things she shouldn't, and was alert to every superstition and old-religion belief of the Negroes. She was a special pet of Pegg's, always getting treats from her in exchange for information. I know Pegg used her against me.

No matter. I'd deal with Pegg and Anne both.

John ushered them up the stairs.

I waited until I heard them running through the hall overhead, screeching and laughing like the little barbarians they were. Pa spoiled them, let them all run wild. No wonder Mama was going daft.

Then I heard the creaking of the dry-well door as it opened. I turned.

Mama stood there, shivering so she couldn't stop. She'd catch the ague if I didn't warm her, just like I'd had to warm baby Edward.

I grabbed her by the shoulders, which felt thinner than they looked. "Mama, come on out of there right now," I ordered.

She obeyed. I slammed the door shut. The keys jingled when she handed them to me, she was shaking so. Quickly I locked the door.

She came along. Abovestairs I put her in the front parlor, where a fire burned in the hearth. I wrapped her in a blanket. Lordy, I was tired of a sudden. I wished somebody would sit me down and wrap me in a blanket and give me something comforting to drink.

I didn't know how much longer I could continue like this, protecting Mama from herself, waking nights when I heard her walking the halls, and getting up to guide her back to bed, before she wandered outside. Wondering when I'd find her one night in the fancy English garden, baying at the moon. Or when I'd wake one fine morning to find baby Edward dead in his cradle.

And trying to keep the knowledge from the other children that our mother was slowly going mad.

And from Pa.

I was fearful that if Pa knew, he'd put her in the asylum in Williamsburg. MyJohn had told me about it. "God's shoe buckles!" he'd said. "They put chains on the people there. They put them in tiny cells. It's a foul bedlam."

"You've seen it?" I'd asked.

"No, but I've heard."

"That won't do for Pa. As a lawyer, he'll say it's secondhand information. That we must see for ourselves."

"Then I'll take you, and you can tell him. As a matter of fact, you're due for a visit to Williamsburg. You've been working too hard around here."

"And visiting the insane asylum will help me?"

"No." He'd grinned. "My friends, the Douglasses, have a new play that opens soon. *The Beggar's Opera.* We'll go see the asylum first, then the play and supper. You can stay with Mrs. Rind. I'll go to an inn. It'll cheer you, if the asylum casts you down."

He didn't shilly-shally about things. Oh, I needed him now. I wanted to see him this very minute. I loved him so! The breadth of his shoulders, his strong neck that held up that noble head, his blond curly hair, his hard jawline and straight nose and gentle mouth.

I believed in God when I looked at him, more than when I read the Bible.

Was that blasphemy? Never mind, I didn't care.

I'd go with MyJohn to see the asylum. I'd do anything to keep Mama out of there. I'd lie, I'd steal, I'd run somebody through the heart with a sword like Charles Chiswell's son did.

I fetched some brandy from the sideboard and gave the glass to Mama. She drank it down quick. I gave her more. I'd get her drunk if I had to, if it would becalm her.

Soon she settled down. There was no sound but the ticking of the clock, the distant screeching of my brothers and sisters outside on the long sloping lawn, running barefoot now. They sounded worse than the Powhatan Indians. They were playing with Pegg's children. My little sisters were rolling down the hill, skirts flying, like hellions.

Anne and Pegg's Nancy were the same age. And I couldn't separate them. Will, Shadrack, and Reuben were poking sticks at a beehive they'd gotten down from a tree. Serve them right if they were all stung to pieces. I saw John trying to take the stick away from them.

John couldn't be expected to mind them for long. He was a young man already, coming into a young man's estate. I knew he wanted to ride over this afternoon to see Dorothea Dandridge. She was the daughter of one of the most esteemed families around here. Her father was a man of large means. His mother, wed to the late Governor Spotswood. They had parties all the time in their mansion house, card games, minuets, even marches in the ballroom. Pa had known Dorothea since she was four.

John was smitten with her. But Pa did not know it. And I knew he would disapprove. John was only a gangling youth, after all, with nothing to offer Dorothea. It would only lead to heartbreak.

More than once I'd wanted to tell Pa of John's secret rides over there. John'd begged me not to. So had Anne, who took his part in everything.

Still, John had other fish to fry. He had a tutor to answer to, studies, and his horses. John was set on raising horses and planned to run his filly, Small Hope, in the Sweepstakes Race this August. I was hoping that his love of racing and breeding would make him forget Dorothea in time.

I didn't like being the oldest. And I needed MyJohn's steady voice and firm hand around here all the time. Pa's already asked us to live here when we wed in a year. Why not sooner?

I determined to push for our wedding. I might be only sixteen, but Mama was sixteen when she wed Pa, wasn't she? And he only eighteen? Didn't he always tell me I was his favorite? The one he depended on? The glue that held the family together?

Behind me I heard Mama whimper and then sigh. I turned. She was asleep.

I must talk to Pegg. Make sure she didn't speak of what she'd seen. There was another problem, the Negroes.

MyJohn came over every day now, to help our manager, David Melton, keep the place running. He even kept the books for Pa. We had near seventy Negroes on the place altogether. And things were changing all around.

MyJohn said there were more and more whisperings amongst the field people. I knew Pegg was getting bolder and bolder. So were Alice and Silvy. MyJohn said the field Negroes were gathering in groups, sloughing off work, and giving David a lot of sass of late.

Every white planter's family in the commonwealth was afraid of their Negroes.

Pa and I had spoken often of the problem.

"If war comes, I have no doubt that the British will encourage slave insurrections to discourage a patriot movement," Pa said.

Pa's been talking about war for a whole year now, in meetings.

They call Pa the Voice in those meetings. Mr. Jefferson, the Pen. And Colonel Washington, the Sword.

Pa says he hates slavery.

But he also says he's drawn along by the inconvenience of living in Virginia without his Negroes. "But a time will come when we can abolish this evil. Until then, we can at least treat them with leniency," he says.

So there it was. Pa's Negroes must be treated with leniency. He'd talked with MyJohn, David Melton, and me about it. We all promised to abide by his wishes.

But I know that since Mama took her turn for the worse, Pegg has decided to test her mettle. And mine. If it weren't for Mama, I'd wed MyJohn and go and live with him and write poetry, as I like to do. And visit Williamsburg during Publick Times, when General Court is held, and attend balls and lectures, the fairs and the theater. And then come home and have babies.

But for now I am needed here. I sat down on the floor and leaned my head against Mama's chair as she dozed. She'd walked again last night, and I knew she was pure spent and would sleep the afternoon away. The fire crackled. I plotted.

Chapter Two

———

BECAUSE PA READ and loved John Locke, he believed in Mr. Locke's theory that a child can "play
himself into learning."

He let the little ones run wild about the plantation.
They came home with scratched legs and dirty faces.
Anne had ruined so many dresses, I couldn't keep up with
their repair. It kept me from working on my dowry
linens, and I loved working on them.

When we could get them in the house, Will and Anne
were supposed to be tutored afternoons by Mr. Chitwell,
John's tutor. John's lessons were done by midday. But
many an afternoon Mr. Chitwell waited for Anne and
Will in the front parlor, staring at the imported mahogany
hardwood paneling. And they never came.

After lessons, Anne was to make herself available to
me, to learn the womanly arts so she could look well to
the ways of her household when she grew up.

But Anne had other concerns, mostly having to do

with hanging about Pegg in the kitchen and learning the use of herbs. I didn't want to know what else she was learning, but I suspected it had to do with less-than-savory beliefs.

Yesterday she'd told me how the late Emperor of Russia lost his life. It had to do with a dagger in the throat.

I loved my sister Anne. She could be sweet, and we both enjoyed talking about books and poetry. But she was causing me more and more vexation of late, going in her own direction.

"With all due respect to your father, Miss Patsy, never have I seen such ungovernable children," Mr. Chitwell said on parting that day.

I sighed. "I know. Tomorrow they will be here. I promise."

I stood on the front steps and waved him off. Then waited for the post rider coming up the lane. Oh, what a fine day! I breathed in the spring air, greeted the post rider, and called for Silvy to bring him a cup of cold lemonade. He drank it under the huge oak tree, left the cup on a rock, and waved.

There was a letter from Pa.

I took the mail, newspapers, and letters and walked the long central hall, out the back door. Here I sat on a bench in my newly planted herb garden.

I ripped open the letter.

Good Morrow, Sarah, Daughter, Son,
and little ones:

I write to tell you that I'll arrive home late tonight. Don't wait up. Keep a candle in the

window of the traveler's room, and some cold
meat on the hunter's sideboard. I miss you all.

I folded the letter.

Pa coming home tonight! What would I do? I put the
letter down and filled my eyes with familiar things that
settled me.

There. Some bridal wreath already blooming at the
end of the gardens.

There. Daffodils nodding their yellow heads along the
lane that led through the dependencies, the warehouse,
washhouse, ash house, kitchen, and blacksmith shop.

There, too. Blue field pansies, so pleasing to the eye.

And there! MyJohn coming home from the fields. I
watched him dismount his horse, Peaches, and hand the
reins to Barley, the stableboy. My eyes feasted on the tall
figure he cut, his graceful, sure movements, his elegant
stature as he walked into the detached kitchen to wash.

My favorite fancy was that MyJohn and I were already
wed, and this was our house.

He came out of the kitchen, holding his planter's hat,
his dusty boots making long strides on the lane.

"You look spent. And you're early," I said.

He kissed me. Greedily. I didn't want it to stop, but I
pulled away. Servants were always watching, and deco-
rum must be kept.

"You sound like a wife already. I couldn't wait to see
you."

"Then I'm glad you came early. Have you seen the
children?"

He laughed. "They're running wild with the dogs over Chiswell's grave."

"Did you scold them?" Sometimes MyJohn was too lenient. It was why they liked him so.

"I told them to come home."

"Pegg tells them stories about Chiswell's ghost," I said. Chiswell was buried on the grounds. After bail and before his trial, he'd killed himself. But at the burial, a crowd of men demanded that the casket be opened to make sure Chiswell was really in it.

"Wait until I get my hands on Anne," I said.

"Don't be harsh with her. She's still just a child," MyJohn said. We went to the dining room, where Silvy was just setting down the silver chocolate pot and china cups.

"Anne said that your mother near drowned Edward this morning."

"I knew she'd mouth it all over the place!"

He leaned forward, toward me. "Patsy, your mother is in a perilous way. You can't keep it quiet anymore."

Tears came to my eyes. "You would have me tell Pa?"

"It's his concern, Patsy, not yours."

"It's my job to protect her. I'm the oldest."

He took my hand. "It's your job, dearest, to protect your little brother Edward. And maybe the others. As a gentleman, a man of prominence and honor, your father would take great exception to your not telling him. Did you not think of that?"

I gulped back my tears. "Pegg locked Mama in the dry well. And she turns Anne against me."

"Dearest, that's part of the problem. Pegg senses the mistress of the house is in a weak position, and she's taking over. I can help you with that. I'll speak to her."

"No. I must speak with her. If I don't, she'll never respect me."

He squeezed my hand. "All right. But we must do what's best for Aunt Sarah."

We were cousins. He loved Mama, too. "MyJohn, I'm thinking I should ask Pa if we could wed sooner than next year. Then you can live here and run the place for him."

"David is doing a fine job. I wouldn't usurp his place."

"Are you saying you don't want to wed me sooner?"

A new place was cut into my heart every time he smiled. He smiled now. "You know I'd marry you tomorrow if your father said yes. And I'd continue to work with David. With six hundred acres now cleared, he needs help managing."

He was so dear. "It's the children. We should be here to care for them. Anne runs wild. So does Will. And little Betsy looks to me," I said.

"Ask him, then. I'd gladly help you manage the house and children as well. You know they love me. John asks my advice all the time about his horses. He needs a man to talk to on occasion."

"Pa's coming home late tonight."

"Good."

From the back entrance came the shrieking of children. I stood up. "I must go."

"And I must see to the books before supper." He held on to my hand as we walked to the back entrance, where the children were wiping their muddy feet with pieces of burlap. Pegg and her Nancy were with them. Anne was forever bringing Nancy into the house. She'd take her to her room, if I'd let her.

Anne was not a pretty child. Too thin of face, yet her hair, which was strawberry colored and thick and always flying loose, gave her the appearance of a fairy child. Her eyes were as blue as the field pansies. She gave you a turn, all right. She had more intelligence than any girl had a right to have. It would bring her to trouble if she didn't keep it in tow.

"Anne, where have you been?" I demanded. "Look at you. You look like a wanton."

"What's a wanton?"

"Never mind. Go upstairs and change. No, wait."

She turned. "MyJohn says you were running over Chiswell's grave with the dogs."

Pegg took Nancy and the dirty burlap and went outside.

"We don't run over people's graves, Anne. We respect the dead."

"He's not in the grave."

"What? Who told you such nonsense? Pegg?"

"Pegg says he's not in the coffin. He wanted to be buried here, but he isn't. And so his ghost haunts the place."

"That's folderol. There's no such thing as ghosts."

"There are. Pegg says he comes whenever there's a full moon. And next full moon, I'm going out to see him."

"Did Pegg also tell you not to come to lessons or your household learning?"

She made a face. "Household learning grinds at my innards." Then her face brightened. "I saw a white pigeon on one of the chimneys. That means calamity is near." Anne was taken with calamity. It presented her with opportunities.

MyJohn went to her, knelt down close, and whispered something in her ear. She smiled. Then he stood. "Now go upstairs and get clean, as your sister says. You, too, Will."

They went. Will adored MyJohn. Times they acted like he was around for their benefit, not mine.

They ran. Then halfway up, Anne stopped. "Is Mama all right?"

"She's doing well," I lied.

She made a face. "Calamity's coming. I knew it when I saw the white pigeon."

"Anne." MyJohn's voice was gentle.

I leaned on MyJohn's shoulder. "Pa says I'm the glue that holds this family together. What holds the glue together?"

He kissed me again. "Love."

Oh, what would I do without him?

———

I SET WILL to reading and Anne to working on her sampler before supper. Betsy, I put down for a nap. Mama woke long enough to nurse Edward, then both went back to sleep again. The house settled under the waning sun.

Then I walked outside to the kitchen to speak to Pegg.

Once Pegg had held me on her lap when I was a child, rocked me, soothed me, told me stories, bathed and dressed me. Her strong arms had been my refuge.

When I'd been invited to other plantations for balls or routs or barbecues, it was Pegg who'd accompanied me. But it is a sign of growing up to distance yourself from the Negroes.

There comes a time in every white child's life when you must let them know you are in charge. It is, for some of us, the most difficult thing to do.

"Mama will be at the board for supper," I told Pegg. She was basting the ham. "Good."

"I want no mention of this morning. She's forgotten it."

She made a sound in her throat. I saw Silvy and Alice exchange glances, which meant she'd told them all about it.

I took a step forward from the doorway. "Pegg, you locked Mama in the dry well again. I won't have it."

She was putting butter in the peas. "It makes her come round, doan it?"

"That is not for you to decide! And if you do it again, I'll tell Pa."

"Seems to me you oughta tell him anyways."

"Don't sass me, Pegg. I won't have it!" My voice cut the air like a knife slicing butter.

Her eyes flicked down. "Yes, Miss," she said.

I looked at Alice and Silvy. They, too, dropped their gaze to the floor.

I turned to go. "And please stop telling Anne ghost stories and encouraging her to disobey me."

"Uh-huh," she agreed.

Leaving, I was stopped by her voice. "You oughta get a wet nurse for Edward."

"What?"

"Seems to me, if'n your mama got her mind set to drown him, you oughta let somebody else nurse him."

God's shoe buckles, as MyJohn would say. Why hadn't I thought of that? "Who?" I asked.

"Delia gonna give birth any hour now. Seems to me you oughta think on it."

"Of course. I was giving the matter thought," I said. And I walked out the door.

Supper was a quiet affair, with the children on their best behavior. Even little Betsy sat at table with us. I read a piece from the Bible before we ate, as Pa would want me to do.

I hadn't told Mama that Pa was coming home yet, and cautioned the children not to, either. But now it was time to tell her. I did it gently.

"Pa's coming home tonight." I put my hand over hers. "He sent word."

"Your pa? Why, darling, Pa died. Don't you remember? He took sick at the Charlotte County Courthouse. A blockage of the bowels. Dr. Cabell gave him a vial of liquid mercury as a last resort. And it killed him."

"Mama!" I gasped. The children started to whimper. "Hush," I told them. "Pa's not dead. Mama just had a bad dream. Silvy, take them to the front parlor, and we'll read before bedtime."

She did so.

"Mama," I turned to her again. "We live in Hanover County. What would Pa be doing in the Charlotte County Courthouse?"

"Why, darling, we lived there when he took sick. And

when he offered himself as a candidate for a seat in the House of Delegates."

"You mean the House of Burgesses, Mama."

"No, dear, the House of Delegates." She smiled. "This is after he was elected governor for the sixth time."

She was predicting things now. Was that all part of it? I took her hand. "Mama, Pa can never be governor. He's a colonial. And accused of treason, remember?"

She patted my hand. "He was governor six times. Now I'm tired. I think I'll retire. Will you see to the children?"

I did not look at MyJohn. But I knew the pain that would be written on his face. I said yes, I would see to the children.

Chapter Three

———

"YOUR MA HAS the sight," Pegg told me that night. "The Lord is restorin' to her for what the locust hath eaten."

How like Pegg to say something like that. The Negroes believed in things like second sight and uncommon powers. We paid no mind to their nonsense.

We were in the little clapboard house next to the mansion house, where Pa did his law work when he was home. Where MyJohn went to keep the books. Upstairs there were two bedrooms for any law clerks Pa might bring with him. I had Pegg put fresh sheets on the beds and I swept the place out. I neatened Pa's desk and put fresh ink in the bottle. I sharpened his quill pens.

"She sees nothing," I shot back. "She's just raving."

"Mark her words," Pegg pushed. "The addled have the sight sometimes. Who are we to say who is sane and who isn't?"

I locked up Pa's office.

"You want I should get the cold meat and leftover biscuits an' fix things in the traveler's room?" she asked.

I said no. I wanted to do that for Pa myself. I sent her to the quarters for the night, then fetched the food and brought it inside where I set it on the hunter's sideboard and covered it with napkins. Then I lighted a fire.

Everything would be perfect for Pa. The traveler's room had a brick floor and its own entrance. Pa used it for travelers who came to see him. The brick floor wouldn't be ruined by their muddy boots. I got fruit and Madeira wine ready, too. Pa's tastes were simple.

I lighted candles and set them in the windows. The nights were still chilled. Here in Hanover County many was the time we'd had hailstorms in May, ruining the orchards and crops.

Ma was asleep. Edward was in his cradle in my room. When the fire had warmed the traveler's room, I brought his cradle in, so Pa could see him. Thank heaven he'd started sleeping through the night of late.

I wrapped myself in an old quilt and put a branch candlestick on the table beside me. It was pewter, not silver. Pa's fondness for plainness spilled over to the household furnishings. We still had animal skins on the floors, not Persian carpets, even though ours was one of the biggest houses in the county.

Pa seemed fearful of ostentation. It harkened back to his youth.

When he was a boy, he spent a lot of time with his uncle Langloo Winston, his mother's brother, who'd lived half the time in far-flung wilderness cabins, traded with Indians, and was said to have Indian wives. Great Uncle Langloo never came near polite society in the Tidewater.

Pa's people are all Winstons and Dabneys, educators, writers, military officers. Pa was born knowing he came from eminence, but if he wanted to rise in the world, he had to do it on his own because everything his mother had went to his older half brother, John Syme, Jr., from his mother's first marriage. And his own pa gambles and is a poor manager.

Pa and his brother William had kept a poor-man store and gone bankrupt. Then he married Mama, with me already on the way, and worked in her father's tavern and worked his own fields with the Negroes.

I think, even though he's a famous lawyer now, he's no more than two whoops and a holler from being a backwoodsman himself.

When he first started lawyering, he used to hunt deer, pheasant, and partridge along the way to Louisa Court-house. He'd be wearing his leather breeches. His coat would be stained with blood from the hunt. He'd go into the courthouse to take up a case with a brace of ducks in his hands and his saddlebags on his arms.

I think that's why Anne is the little savage she is, that she takes after Uncle Langloo.

Well, I was doing my best with Anne. I settled in the chair, thinking it was time I started her on the loom. For three years now we've been planting flaxseed, and Pa got us a loom and flax sickle, and we wear homespun.

I miss my silk, but I still have six yards of crimson laid

by. I wondered if Pa would mind if I sewed up a gown of it. As Patrick Henry's daughter, would that be unpatriotic? MyJohn so likes me in silk. I wondered if I should bother telling Pa? I could wear it after we were wed, when we had parties. A girl had a right to silk in her dowry chest, didn't she? Still, I mustn't let Anne see me working on it. She'd tell.

I picked up the tea towels from my dowry chest that I'd brought to work on. Outside there was a near-full moon. When it came on to being full, Anne would be outside at Chiswell's grave, waiting to see his ghost. She was good for her promises.

An owl somewhere in a tree was asking who. At my feet was Pa's best hunting dog, Charger, who was getting long in the tooth and spent nights near the fire.

What would it be like, I wondered, to be married? To nevermore have to say good-bye to MyJohn? To have him with me always?

Why did Pa, who was so ahead of everybody else in his thinking, have such set ideas about a wife's place in the scheme of things? Maybe that's why Mama was going mad. He believed a woman should never try to control her husband by opposition, displeasure, or anger.

Mama hadn't. I never recollect her trying to oppose him. When they wed in the front parlor of her father's house at Rural Plains, she'd promised to obey him "even as Sarah obeyed Abraham, calling him Lord."

I could not be that kind of wife. Nor would MyJohn want me to be.

If Pa had only made more allowances for her. If only

he'd shown the same compassion as he had for criminals in the Court of Oyer and Terminer in Williamsburg. And what about the time he rode fifty miles to defend a Baptist minister imprisoned in Spotsylvania County jail? He'd charged into the courtroom. "Great God!" he'd yelled. "Did I hear what those men are charged with? What? Preaching the gospel of the Son of God? Did I hear that?"

The case was dropped.

Would he yell "Great God!" when he heard about Mama?

Pa was not mean to her. He never struck her, never even raised his voice. I know he loves her. But he's become so much of a *personage* now. Arguing all those cases, presenting all those resolutions.

"Your passions are no longer your own when he addresses them," George Mason, a friend of George Washington, had said of Pa after hearing him speechify.

Nor is your reason, I thought.

I worked on my tea towels until Charger thumped his tail, got up, and went, whining, to the door. Pa was home.

HE CAME IN quietly. His blue eyes took in the room, the cradle, me. I knew he was looking for Mama.

"Patsy," he said. And in one fluid movement he patted Charger's head, dropped his saddlebags, set his cloak aside, and reached out to me.

"Pa, I'm glad you're home." I tried not to let my voice break. I needed to be strong. He disliked weakness.

He hugged me fiercely, and I felt as if *I*'d come home, not him.

His face was rough with a day's growth of beard. He smelled of tobacco and horse.

"Sit, Pa, I've got food. Sit by the fire. Is the wind picking up?"

He sat, but not before leaning down to touch little Edward's face. The baby stirred and in his sleep made a suckling motion with his mouth. "He's grown," Pa said.

"Yes. He's thriving." I fixed a plate of meat and biscuits, butter, cheese, and pickled preserves. I served a glass of Madeira.

"Ah, Patsy, you spoil me." He sat, setting his tricorn hat down. Again the piercing blue eyes under his bushy brows took in the room. "Where's your mother?"

"In bed."

He ate. But he was interested in food only for the nourishment it gave his body. He'd as soon eat coon as ham or turkey.

"Did you bring any clerks with you?" I asked.

"No. I'll be off to Chesterfield County in two days."

"Oh, Pa!" I wailed, but his look stopped me. The sudden scowl, the strong mouth gone grim, the firm chin and high forehead and long nose. That face had stopped better people than me, I told myself.

It had stopped Parliament and the Stamp Act, hadn't it?

"Another Baptist preacher in trouble," he said. "The minister of the parish ruined the preacher's Bible with the butt end of his riding whip, then shoved the whip into the preacher's mouth. Then the clerk of the court roped him to his horse and dragged him to the sheriff, who gave him twenty lashes. We can't have such persecution, Patsy."

"Are you the only one to come to their defense?"

"I've become their Robin Hood, it seems." He shook his head. "How can we have a prosperous land if we don't encourage religious toleration?"

He'd be speechifying soon, if I didn't stop him.

"Pa," I said, "Mama is ill."

He gulped down his Madeira. "What do you mean, 'ill'? Ague? Fever? What?"

"Her mind, Pa," I said gently. "Her mind goes. This morning she had a spell."

"'A spell'?"

"She tried to drown Edward."

He put aside his plate and glass. The fire spit. I waited. He got up and went again to kneel beside the cradle to touch the baby's head. "Is he all right?"

"Yes."

"God save us." He stood and looked at me. "So you know."

"What?" I asked.

"What think you, Patsy? She is my wife. I've known for a while now."

"That she wanted to kill Edward?"

"That she was sad and weeping all the time. But I thought it was just what sometimes comes after a birth. Not this." He gestured to the cradle. "Are the other children all right?"

"Right as rain, Pa. But Anne saw it."

He shook his head.

"Why didn't you say something to me, Pa?"

"I wanted to, but betimes I thought I was wrong. I prayed I was wrong." He came over to me, put his hand on my head. "I've been a coward," he said.

I looked up at him. "You, a 'coward'? You who spoke treason against the king?"

He turned away. "This is a new turn, this business about harming the baby." His shoulders slumped. "Though I had no idea she had come to such a dolorous state, I've already taken some steps."

"What 'steps'?" My heart pounded.

"I've spoken to Dr. Pasteur and Dr. Galt in town. They recommend Dr. Hinde. He's coming to see her tomorrow." He sat down. He did not look at me. "Pasteur and Galt spoke of a place in Williamsburg, if she got any worse." He stared into the fire.

"Pa!"

"What else?" His voice grew strong in the way that robbed you of your passions and your reason.

"It's a terrible place," I whispered. "MyJohn told me about it. He offered to take me to see it."

"She'd be kept away from the vagrants. But yes, you go with MyJohn to see it. Mr. Pelham, the jail keeper, said his wife, Mary, would personally see to her."

"The jail keeper," I said dully.

"Would you have the little ones see her worsen?"

Silence, deep and swirling, like the New Found River after it rained hard. Then he spoke. "It's all we have until the hospital is finished in Williamsburg, for those with ailments of the mind. The House of Burgesses has approved Mr. Pelham's accommodations."

No sense in arguing. Not with a man who charges into court and gets cases dropped.

"MyJohn and I will go tomorrow," I said. "We'll stay with Mrs. Barrow, Clementina Rind's sister, on the road, then Clementina can put me up one night while we are there. Is that all right with you?"

"Better than camping in the woods," he said dourly. He camped out on the two-day ride to Williamsburg when the weather permitted.

"When do you leave?"

"When you get back will be all right."

"Pegg says we should get a wet nurse for Edward. She reminded me that Delia is about to give birth."

"That might be a good idea. Would you see to it?"

I kissed him. "Yes," I said.

Nobody knows him like I do, I thought. He is so forceful and powerful in court, because there he meets the enemy, injustice, and can overcome it. But here at home he cannot name the enemy. It is not in any resolves or writs or law books.

It wasn't until I'd climbed into bed that I remembered that I'd not asked him about my wedding.

Chapter Four

———

ALWAYS I'D GONE with Mama to Williamsburg. To Margaret Hunter's Shoppe, on Duke of Gloucester Street, where I'd gotten my new riding habit.

Before we'd stopped importing English goods, that is.

We'd have tea and cakes in the bake shop of the Raleigh Tavern.

When we still drank tea.

Or, better, visit Clementina Rind at the *Gazette* office. Her coffee and gingerbread were much more enticing.

Clementina was a special friend to our family. Although I found her rather pushy for a female. But, I supposed, if you helped your husband run the newspaper, you had to be pushy.

Many a harried housewife or romantic maid betook of her coffee and gingerbread and hospitality. It wasn't only that she wrote stories, as well as women's news, recipes, gossip, and notices. She encouraged budding poets and gave advice: from the latest news of proper mourning clothes to when the Hampton post rider would arrive from York-town to Williamsburg (Tuesdays and Saturdays).

MyJohn was wise enough to know I needed a woman friend to talk to, pushy or not, and dropped me off.

"Patsy Henry, how good to see you." She came to the front room herself to greet me, wiping ink-stained hands on her apron. "I've got your room all ready."

I sank down by the large multipaned window that was hung with prints from England showing the latest fashions.

In the background hovered William and John, six and eight, and Maria, her small daughter. Her older boys, Charles and James, helped in the shop. And the Rinds supported an older relative, John Pinkney; an apprentice, Isaac Collins; and a Negro named Dick.

"I have that magazine your mama asked for last time she was in."

"Mama's not well," I said.

She nodded knowingly. "Come to the back. I have coffee and gingerbread."

As she poured coffee, the look in her amber eyes quickened. "I saw, last time she was here, that she was sad and distracted. Sometimes that happens to women after a baby."

"My mother is going mad, Clementina," I told her.

Nothing surprised her. "Last time, she told me how sorry she was that my husband had died. And how brave I was to take over the shop."

I nodded. "That's part of it. She speaks of the future.

She says Pa is dead, too. She tried to drown little Edward. She tried to take off her clothes in the garden."

"Does your father know?"

"He says we must do something. He's thinking of putting her in the part of the jail that is for the sick of mind."

"You must not put her there, Patsy. The news yesterday was that a man from North Carolina came to claim a runaway slave in the jail. The slave had a broken leg and was covered with lice."

"But what to do, then?"

"Mr. Hay, who was once owner of the Raleigh Tavern, died of cancer in Prince Edward County, where he'd been staying with a Mrs. Woodson, who is famous for the cures she has discovered for various disorders. Her care is excellent."

"You mean we should send Mama away?"

"It would be better than Mr. Pelham's care."

"Pa would never allow it. He wants her near."

"What about the cellar in your home, then?"

I supposed that went with being a pushy woman. She didn't shilly-shally.

"Your mama showed the cellar to me once. I recollect it as being commodious and well lighted, with windows to let in the air."

"We have eight rooms belowstairs, yes," I said.

"Then that is the place for your mother. You must go and see this asylum today. Your intended is a good man. He'll convince your father it's no place for your mother. Then you must make your father think it is his idea to put her in the cellar."

"Oh, Clementina, thank you. I feel better already."

She walked me to the stairway. "You know which room it is. Oh yes, we've had heated arguments run in the paper with those who still import English goods. Now we're going to publish the names of locals who are still importing."

I gasped. "Oh, that's a wonderful idea, but wouldn't it cause trouble by making them uncomfortable?"

"It's my job to make certain people uncomfortable. Your neighbor Mrs. Hooper is on the list. I wanted to tell you before you saw it in the paper."

I hated Mrs. Hooper. She was a busybody, always poking her nose in where it didn't belong. She insisted her husband have the family crest painted on their carriage.

"Has anyone heard from Sarah Hallam and Jonathan?" I asked.

"No. That poor girl. If she came to me for help, I'd shelter them. If she comes to you, send her here, Patsy."

Sarah was the niece of Mrs. Hooper. She'd been raised by Mrs. Hooper and her husband, but fallen desperately smitten with Jonathan Snead. Mrs. Hooper had put a notice in the *Gazette*, telling all county clerks not to grant them a marriage license and advising all ministers not to pronounce the banns or to marry them. In the weeks since the announcement, Sarah and Jonathan had run off. Nobody knew where they were.

Clementina gave me a tin of tea for Mama. She kept tea on hand for those who needed it. She gave me a novel, too: *Gulliver's Travels.* "Read it to the little ones," she said.

I went upstairs to my room to change before meeting MyJohn.

———

"HERE'S OUR MOST commodious accommodation, Mr. Fontaine. As you can see, it is clean and bright," Mr. Pelham said.

We were in the basement of the jail-asylum. Though the sun shone outside, here it was dim. Mr. Pelham carried a lantern.

We stood in the doorway of a dolorous-looking room that had one cot covered with ticking. Likely a straw mattress, I told myself. If that.

The rushes on the floor smelled sour. On the way down the stairs, I saw two rats darting about. The walls were brick. Some of the bricks were cracked in many places and dripping with water. And green furry stuff grew all over them.

But worst of all, iron rings were driven into one wall of the room.

"What are those rings for?" I asked.

"Why, Miss Henry, you understand," Mr. Pelham said softly, "betimes this room may have to house murderers, or runaway slaves, who must be contained."

From the room next door came a loud, cackling laugh. " 'Betimes,' he says. Just yesterday they moved out a slave what run here from North Ca'lina. Full of lice he was, an' ravin' 'bout a broken leg."

"Who is that?" I asked.

Mr. Pelham shrugged. "Some unfortunate woman

who's had brain fever for the last six months. Don't listen to her. We moved no runaway from here yesterday."

Well, I thought, so he lies, this man.

"She was a servant in Mr. Wythe's house and says she was driven out of there by a ghost," Mr. Pelham explained.

"'Twas Anne Skipwith who drove me out," the voice continued. "She died birthing. She walks at midnight upstairs in Mr. Wythe's house."

"Quiet, you old biddie!" Mr. Pelham ordered. "Or I'll shackle you!"

"Her husband, Sir Peyton Skipwith, was carry'n on with her sister."

Mr. Pelham used his club to pound on the brick wall. The woman fell silent.

We'd seen enough. I tugged at MyJohn's sleeve.

"Yes, thank you," MyJohn said politely. "I shall report to Mr. Henry."

We started up the stairs. But first we passed the room next door. I looked in.

The woman's dress was in tatters. Her hair was loose and hung in disrepair to her shoulders. Her eyes glittered, with what? Madness? Or fever?

"Lice," she said, "the runaway had lice. Now I've got them in here with me."

We continued up the stairs.

She called after us. "There's a cold spot in the hallway in Mr. Wythe's house. It's where Mrs. Skipwith stands at midnight!"

Behind us Mr. Pelham said, in a pleading voice, "Mrs. Henry would receive the best of care. I'll remove the biddie next door."

Never was I so glad to get out into the sunlight! MyJohn lingered for a moment to speak to Mr. Pelham.

"Are you all right?" he asked as we drove away.

I told him I was. "Clementina told me about the runaway slave taken out yesterday, with lice and a broken leg."

He nodded, and we spoke no more about the place. It was too terrible to contemplate. There was no question in either of our minds of my mother going there. The understanding was like a warm blanket between us.

"I've got tickets for the theater," he said. "And then we'll have supper."

Chapter Five

O UR LONG, RECTANGULAR house, known as
Scotchtown, was shingled with cypress. Candles
glowed in all the windows. Fire burned in iron-rimmed
holders stuck in the ground at each side of the front steps,
where John and Barley waited for us.

"I sense calamity," I told MyJohn as we drove up.

"You're getting like your sister Anne."

But I was right.

"Trouble," John said.

"What?" we both asked.

"Mama had some kind of fit this afternoon. Threw
things around in the front parlor. Then went and did the
same in their chamber. Kept at me to get Pa out of her
sight. Said he was dead and come back to haunt her. I
think she's sick, Patsy."

"God's shoe buckles," MyJohn said.

Young John looked near tears. "The place is a shambles,

and she won't let the Negro servants near her. Says they're going to poison her. The children need you. So does Mama."

I ran inside, MyJohn behind me. In the wide center hall I peered into the front parlor. There I saw broken glass strewn on the floor—the chimney of the candle-holder. Books and newspapers were thrown about, some fruit amongst them. The pianoforte bench was on its side. Two walnut chairs were overturned, the damask curtains half ripped from the windows, and crewelwork pillows tossed about.

"Is Mama all right?" I turned to John.

He shrugged. "Pa's with her."

"Go to the children, MyJohn, please. They take comfort from you. John, ask Silvy or Pegg to fetch some tea to Mama's chamber." I handed him the tin of tea that Clementina had given me.

"She won't let the Negroes near her," John said again.

"Do it!" Both my brother and MyJohn went off. The door to Mama's chamber was a bit open. From inside, candlelight cast Pa's long shadow. He was leaning over the bed. Mama was curled up on it, sobbing.

The room was strewn with every sort of object. Combs and brushes, Pa's boots and coats, the water pitcher and bowl lay broken. Water slopped on the floor, soaking a braided rug. Mama's clothes were half in and half out of the clothespress. The bed hangings were pulled down.

"Come now, Sarah. I'm here, love. Alive," Pa was saying gently. "Alive and come back to you. Please, Sarah, please."

"Pa?"

He looked up, saw me, and seemed relieved. "Patsy."

"What happened?"

"She woke from an afternoon nap and saw me and went into a rage. Said I'm dead and a ghost. Come soothe her, Patsy, I must see to the children."

"I sent MyJohn to talk to them. And Pegg's bringing Mama some tea."

Mama heard that and sat up. Her cap was off, her long dark hair disheveled, and in her eyes was a look that told me she was somewhere dark and frightening, and privy to secrets she could not tell.

"I won't have Pegg near me. She's been trying to poison me a little bit at a time. They do, you know." She gripped my hand. "It's why I'm ill. She's been slipping liquid mercury into my chocolate and coffee."

I knelt beside the bed. "No, Mama, Pegg would not do that."

She pulled away from me. "Nobody believes me," she said.

"All right, Mama. We believe you." I looked up at Pa, and he nodded in agreement. Anything to allay her fears.

"You weren't here," she moaned. "I looked for you."

"I went to Williamsburg with MyJohn."

"Williamsburg? How is Clementina doing since her husband died? She told me he left debts of more than fifteen hundred pounds."

"He didn't die, Mama. He's alive and well."

"Have the citizens attacked the Governor's Palace?" She was so agitated! "Mama," I said, "nobody has died and nobody is attacking anybody." Just then Pegg appeared in the doorway with the tray of tea. Before Mama could see her, I quickly took the tray and motioned her away. Then I turned to Pa.

"I've got her some tea, Pa. I know you don't approve, but it will settle her."

He waved his hand, giving me permission.

"You've missed your tea, haven't you? Clementina Rind sent it."

"They've sided with the British, you know. The Negroes. They'll kill us in our beds. They are posted as guards outside the Governor's Palace! Oh, the tea smells wonderful."

She drank and closed her eyes. "I've missed my tea so." And while she drank, she spoke. "This place is haunted. And Chiswell's ghost isn't the only one. Indians raided it once. I hear their war cries at night. Indians are going to make war on the frontier soon again. You must write to Aunt Annie and Colonel Christian and tell them to come home."

Pa's sister, Aunt Annie, and her husband, Colonel Christian, who'd fought in the Seven Years War, lived over the mountains in Indian territory.

"The Indians are not attacking now, Mama."

"They will, they will. The stain of blood on the hall floor is not only from that duel. There is a curse on this place. I feel it." She looked up at Pa.

"It's the ghost of your pa again. He won't give me any peace."

"It's no ghost, Mama. It's really Pa."

"Tell his ghost I want to go back to Roundabout."

It was the last place they'd owned. In Louisa County.

"This is our home now, Sarah," he told her. "You love this place."

"Don't tell me what I love and what I don't love," she said. "The British will soon ride through this house. On horses."

Pa was pure shaken.

I got up and closed the door. "I'll give her some laudanum," I whispered. "Go see that Silvy gets the children ready for bed. MyJohn can stay the night, if needed. Ask him."

He nodded, got up, patted me on the shoulder, and whispered in my ear. "We must talk this night, Patsy. Come to the traveler's room after she goes to sleep. Bring MyJohn and your brother."

I said yes, I would.

———

FOR A WILD moment after I settled Mama down, I wondered: What if she is right? What if Pegg is poisoning her, little by little, with liquid mercury?

What about that group of slaves who'd poisoned several overseers in Fairfax County just a couple of years back?

And what about John Knox's people murdering him over in Stafford County? And Bowler Cock's Negroes fighting against whites in his barn two years past?

Then I thought, no. Pegg has been with us for years. I can't go down that hole with Mama. If I do, I'm as mad as she is.

But what if it is so?

I mopped up the floor where water had spilled. I straightened the bed hangings. I picked up the broken pieces of the pitcher and water bowl and tiptoed out to bring it to the kitchen. I crept back into Mama's room to set the rest of it straight.

She was sleeping.

Something was stirring in my mind. I could never forgive myself if Mama's words were true about Pegg poisoning her and I didn't heed them. So I decided to take some sips of the tea.

If there was liquid mercury in it, I'd become sick, but I wouldn't die.

It was the least I could do for Pa and the others.

I heard the children and MyJohn in the hall. He was ushering them into the outside kitchen for warm milk and cookies. Quickly I poured some tea from the pot into Mama's cup and put in some sugar. Then I raised the cup to my lips and sipped it.

It had no special taste. But such a small quantity of liquid mercury wouldn't.

I gulped the rest of it down. Lordy, I missed my tea! I might just have a real cup of it later on tonight. I deserved it, didn't I? Who but I was holding this family together?

Then I tidied myself to meet Pa and the others in the traveler's room.

———

"I WANT TO discuss what to do with your mother." Pa stood in front of the hearth, hands behind his back, like he was in the House of Burgesses. He looked wan. Lines were in his face I had never paid mind to before.

The three of us settled to listen.

"I have decided that she must be put in some place. To be cared for. I do not want the children to see her like this."

"Where, Pa?" I asked.

"That depends on what intelligence you two have for me from Williamsburg."

"Sir, Patsy and I found the asylum to be in disarray and filth. And Mr. Pelham lied to us," MyJohn said.

Pa raised his eyebrows. "How so?"

MyJohn explained. Pa listened and nodded.

"And after Patsy left," MyJohn added, "I asked him about food. He said it's mostly pease porridge and small beer."

"Thank you," Pa said. And then, "No, no, of course, we can't put her there. But where?"

Nobody answered. Pa was thinking out loud. "I've heard of a woman in Prince Edward County. But I wouldn't want her that far away."

"If," I ventured, "she could be kept somewhere here. On this place. Out of sight of the children. Then she could be well cared for."

He looked at me sternly, and I fell silent. "Now, where could I keep her here," he demanded, "that the children wouldn't see or hear her? You know they poke into every inch of this place."

"But the place is so big!" I pushed.

Please God, I prayed, let him come to it. Please.

He was pacing again. Then finally he did.

"The cellar," he said. "Didn't you tell me, Patsy, that Pegg confined her in the cellar?"

"In the dry well," I said. "But it's freezing in there, Pa, though there are other rooms."

"I know that." He was still stern. "We could possibly put her there, cared for by Pegg."

"She hates Pegg," John put in.

I poked him in the ribs with my elbow, but Pa waved that problem off. "That's today. Tomorrow she'll hate someone else." He stopped pacing. "So it's what we'll do, then. MyJohn, John, come with me there now. I'll have to leave directions for you. For what is needed to make a room commodious enough for her. Then I'll have to count on you to fix it up."

They started out of the room. "Patsy, you've done enough." Pa turned to me. "Go to bed, child. You look spent."

Before I took myself off to my room, I checked on Mama. She was sleeping peacefully.

In the hall I found Pegg, locking up for the night. "Fetch me some hot water, cream, and sugar," I directed. "I wish to give Mama another cup of tea."

I went to my chamber and bent over little Edward in his cradle. He'd stay with me tonight. He was wide-awake and smiled at me. Oh, such a beautiful child! What would become of him, I wondered. Why, MyJohn and I would raise him as our own!

I prepared for bed, then sat by a lone candle for a while and tried to read my Bible. Pegg knocked and came in with the tray.

"You wants me to bring it to her?"

"No," I said. "She won't have you about her right now. Says you're about to poison her."

Pegg set the tray down. "How she come to that, your mama? I been servin' her fer years. I one o' the Negroes her daddy gave her when she wed."

"I know that," I said. "She's sick in the mind, Pegg. Don't take on so."

She left. And I poured the tea and fixed it the way I liked it and sat back in bed, savoring the flavor. But the full joy of it was lost thinking on Mama.

Up until now everything had been coming at me too fast, like an Indian arrow, straight and true. But now the truth had struck about her, and the wound was starting to bleed.

Mama might never be right again. She might, forever, be in our cellar, ranting about Indian attacks, the Negroes trying to poison us, and telling me who had died.

How could this be?

She had always been soft-spoken and regal, loving and gentle. With Pa away so much, she was the only one we had to turn to.

She liked to make tarts and fill them with jams. Once Pa became a famous lawyer, she could have sat on her tuffet and eaten curds and whey, as the nursery rhyme went. Stayed out of the kitchen. But no, she went on, baking her favorite things, sewing, even running outside and playing with the children.

What had happened, then? People's mamas didn't just

start drowning their babies and throwing things and making predictions.

What would I do without my mama on my wedding day? How could I not look to her, when she was still alive?

I put the Bible aside. I could not pray. I did not know if I could ever pray again.

I blew out the candles and rolled myself into a ball of misery. It wasn't until I was dozing off did I remember the tea. And mind that I'd not become sick from it.

I almost wished that I would become sick this night. I fell asleep praying that I would, to a God I no longer knew was there. Because if I did, then it would mean Mama was not mad, after all.

Chapter Six

——

I DID NOT GET sick. Though I overslept the next morning. I stood, muddleheaded and gaping at Edward's empty cradle. Fear gripped me, and my head started to throb as I reached for a wrap and ran down the hall to the dining room, where my family was assembled at the table.

"Edward's missing!" I croaked.

I must have looked like an apparition. Like Anne Skipwith, who walked at night in Mr. Wythe's house. I saw MyJohn's eyes go over me. I wondered if I'd leave a cold spot on the floor.

"Delia had her baby during the night," Pa said. "Edward's been taken down to the quarters for nursing."

Of course! I mumbled something about being right back and went to my room to dress. My head felt as if it were filled with cotton. I was benumbed. But I dressed quickly and went back to the dining room.

Anne was about to tell a story. Everyone waited. Pa encouraged the children to speak at meals.

Anne's eyes were sparkling. "It's about divine vengeance," she said importantly.

"Ah, we all could do with a little divine vengeance at breakfast," Pa said. "What better way to start the day?"

I sat down and breathed in the aroma from my coffee as Pegg poured it from over my shoulder.

"It happened late last week over to the Parsons.' Their son Richard was playing at cards in Raleigh Tavern. He wished that if he did not win the next hand his flesh might rot and his eyes never shut."

I took the plate of food that Pegg handed me and saw the approving look on her face as Anne recited her tale.

"Well, he didn't win the game. When he was going to bed he saw a black spot on his leg. Soon the mortification spread all over his body. He died in two days. All his flesh rotted. And nobody could shut his eyes."

"Shameful," I snapped. "Pa, how can you encourage her in such nonsense?"

"It's true," Anne shot back at me.

"Then why wasn't the obituary in the *Gazette*?"

"It's going to be. Soon."

"I just saw Clementina Rind. She said nothing about it."

"Does she tell you everything?" Anne asked haughtily.

"And where did you hear it, then?"

"Pegg told me."

"Pa!" I appealed. "You've got to stop her from lingering

about with Pegg. She picks up the most terrible back-woods tales and ghost stories."

"The children need all the attention they can get these days, Patsy," Pa said. "I'm beholden to Pegg for the time she gives her. I'll always love my uncle Langloo for what he taught me about the woods."

Pegg isn't Uncle Langloo, I thought, but there was no moving Pa once he gave judgment on something. Besides, I'd slept late and been shrewish. That put me out of favor with Pa right off.

"You ought to sit in your mother's place at the table, Patsy," he said to me. His blue eyes found mine, and were level and brooked no argument. He knew me well enough to mind that I wouldn't want to do this. He was punishing me for my impatience with Anne.

I looked at my plate. "I can't."

"I need you to be mistress of the place when I'm gone. If you don't act like a mistress, the Negroes won't obey you."

Across the table we glared at each other. I'd gone up against Pa in the past. But never won. Few did, much less a woman. Everyone fell silent. Then MyJohn got up, went to Mama's chair, and pulled it out for me. Tears came to my eyes, and I took my plate and cup and sat at the head of the table, the other end from Pa.

"It isn't right," I said.

"Many things aren't," Pa agreed. "But we do what we must to keep our lives going. Step-by-step, every day." Then he looked at John. "When your tutor comes, you will have lessons as usual. Afterwards William and Anne will have theirs. It is important that we keep things as normal as possible. I leave after our noon repast, for Chesterfield County. I'll be back before the week is up. And you younger ones are to obey Patsy and MyJohn in everything while I'm away. Am I clear spoken?"

"Yes, Pa," they said in unison.

"I think good Dr. Hinde is riding up the road now. He's going to see to your mama. Stay, stay," he told us. "Remember, keep things as normal as possible. Your mama wants it that way."

———

IN LESS THAN an hour Pa and Dr. Hinde came out of Mama's chamber.

"Miss Patsy." The doctor took my hand in his own. I knew him to be a man of good parts, a father himself, and a friend of Pa's. "Miss Patsy, I am afraid that your mother has taken up residence in her mind in some place that is far from here. Let us hope that it is a good place."

We needed a visit from him to inform us of this? Or did Pa need it, to convince himself he was doing everything he could?

"It is always worse for those who must care for the person. But we must accept it as God's will. Your father's idea of confining her to the cellar with a Negro to care for her is sound and wise. In His own time God will bring her home."

I sniffed and nodded.

"Now, I know some doctors would bleed her to rid her of the bilious humors in her body, but I will not. I have left some laudanum for when she is, shall we say, unmanageable. And Jesuit's bark in the event of fever."

Then he walked outside to his horse, untied it, and stood talking in a low tone with Pa. He mounted and, with a lift of his hat to me, was off.

Only then did I notice Pa's horse being brought around by Barley, the saddlebags already attached.

"You're leaving? Before the noon meal?"

He did not look at me. "I must go, Patsy. The ride is long."

"You always must go." I knew I sounded petulant, but I didn't care.

"It's what I do, Patsy. We need the money."

"Pa, you charged ninety-four fees last year. And you're well on your way to doing better this year."

"You keep track of my cases now?"

"We need you here. The children need you, if only for another hour or so."

"It's more than money, Patsy. People need me. Virginia needs me."

"Mama needs you," I said.

He was fussing with the cinch on his saddle while Barley held the horse by the bridle. He dismissed Barley, then turned to me. "Don't ever argue with me in front of the servants," he said.

I knew I was wrong, but I said nothing.

"You're contentious this morning. I meant to speak to you about your manner with your sister. You are getting too severe with her."

"Pa! Anne is the contentious one! She won't come for

lessons! She roams about all day like a savage, and when she isn't doing that, she's in the kitchen with Pegg, learning the old Negro religion, all superstition and blood. She's sassy and disobedient, and she vexes me whenever she can."

He eyed me. "I thought you and your sister got on uncommon well. All that talk of books and poetry you had between you."

"She's changed."

"Children do. You are the elder. You must give her good example. She has no polite education. I depend on you to teach her innocence and propriety."

"Pa, Anne has as much of that as a water moccasin."

"Which is why you must give her a superiority of understanding. If you expect her to please you, you must appear pleased with her. Don't concern yourself with harmless trifles. She'll come round. I'm depending on you, Patsy."

And who do I depend on? I wondered. My eyes filled with tears.

"You have authority over her because I give it to you," he said. "Authority corrupts, like power. In this instance it will corrupt you, Patsy. It's you I am concerned with."

Oh, he could turn things so his argument always appeared palatable!

"I drank the tea," I told him. "Some of Mama's tea."

He scowled. "I thought we agreed on no tea in this household. I count on you to give good example."

"I drank it because I had to know if Mama was right, if Pegg was poisoning her."

His eyes widened. "Foolish girl," he said. But gently, and in admiration. And I needed that from him now. "You could have become sick."

"I wished for it, Pa. I wished to become sick. It would have meant Mama was not going mad."

He fussed with the cinch again. "You heard the doctor. What's wrong with your mother is not confined to a teacup. And cannot be bled from her."

I did not tell him about my other cup of tea. I never would. "Pa, there's something else."

He waited.

"I want to marry MyJohn."

"You are to wed him."

"I mean sooner than we planned. So he can live here with us. It's more important than ever."

Now he commenced to pick up his horse's hooves, one by one, to examine them. "No, Patsy," he said as he set down the first hoof. "You're too young."

"Mama was wed at sixteen. You were eighteen."

He picked up the second hoof. "Do you think I'm not sensible of the fact that our youthful marriage is a goodly part of what has happened to your mother?"

"Pa, don't say that."

"I shouldn't have to." The third hoof was examined. "Surely, you've watched her over the years, working, sacrificing, bearing children, and being alone with them in my absence."

The fourth hoof. "Some women can remain serene and peaceful in their families. Others need amusing books, plays, balls, assemblies."

"Mama never needed those things."

"How do we know? Because of a youthful marriage and motherhood, she never had them! No, Patsy. Marriage means children, responsibility. You need more time to be young. To enjoy the balls, the routs, the assemblies."

"I'm past that, Pa."

"Well, you shouldn't be." He mounted his horse and sat looking down at me. "I no longer think youthful marriages have anything to recommend them."

"I'm old enough to take care of the young ones in your absence. To run the house."

"But any time you wish a weekend away to accept an invitation, you have it. Let marriage wait, Patsy. Stay young awhile longer. I ask you to wait."

"How long?"

"Two more years."

"Two more years!" I stamped my foot. I looked up at him dismally. "It isn't fair! It was supposed to be one! MyJohn and I love each other! How can you ask us to see each other every day and stay chaste and good?"

"I can because you are my dear girl. And because it is eminently sensible."

You didn't, I wanted to say. You didn't with Mama. But I did not dare.

It came to me then, clear as a bell. "Are you saying what I think you are saying, Pa, that being her daughter, I'll come to Mama's end when I wed and have children?"

He did not answer. "Give yourself more time" was all he said. Then he leaned down and kissed me. "Don't leave baby Edward alone with your mother. Or the other little ones."

"Pa, you can't leave me like this!"

But he was riding off. I watched him. My heart was pounding. "I'm going to drink the rest of the tea!" I yelled after him.

He gave no answer, so I ran down the roundabout after his horse. "I'm going to drink it all! And I don't care about the nonimportation agreements."

He did not turn around. Only waved an arm, dismissing me, as I stood there sobbing.

Chapter Seven

ALL THE REST of that day, Pa's unspoken words worked their way into my blood.

He thought I would turn out like Mama.

Would I? Is that what marriage did to women? I thought of the women I knew. Clementina came to mind first.

She was as sane as a preacher's wife. But then, she worked with her husband. She wrote stories for the paper. She got about and saw people.

Mrs. Hooper, our neighbor? I never liked her, but no, she wasn't daft, only mean as a viper. What about Mrs. Parson, who allowed that rumor to be bandied about concerning her son Richard with the rotted flesh?

I thought about Aunt Annie. She lived in Indian territory, and we'd as yet heard no reports of her mind going.

Then I decided no. It must be only our family. And so I thought again: *It's what Pa meant, truly. It might someday be me.*

I TRIED TO GET away from the sound of the hammering belowstairs. Thank heaven the house was big enough to lose yourself in. And Pa wanted me to be mistress of the place. Very well, I would be.

I must see what Pegg was planning for supper. Cold chicken fricassee, yellow squash, turtle soup, and pound cake for dessert.

It was soap-making time, so I went to cast an eye to Daphne. Her husband, Claye, already had the fire going and was carrying over the water. The key to good soap is the ability to judge the strength of the lye, and use the right portion of grease. I stood, while Claye poured the water over the clean wood ashes and some lime in a barrel and the process was well under way.

Then I went with Silvy, to help her air out the mattress tickings on this beautiful spring day.

I knew I should bring Edward to Delia to be nursed, but I could not bring myself to do that.

"Would you take him down?" I asked Pegg.

She gave me a sly glance. How could I be mistress of the place if I couldn't even visit the quarters? Mama used to go every day to see what was needed, to take care of anyone who was sick, to visit new babies.

I gave Pegg a look, letting her know I would brook no sass from her as I handed my brother over.

"Tell Delia that if she is well enough tomorrow, I expect her up here at the house to nurse him," I said.

"Yes, Miss Patsy." At the door, she turned. "Your mama be cryin' in her room 'cause she can't see the baby. You best let me give her some of my remedies."

"The doctor said laudanum."

"My remedies fix her better."

I gave her no answer. I brought Mama some leftover dinner pudding.

"Where is Edward? Where is my baby?" Her hair was hanging loose about her shoulders. She wore a silk sacque.

"He's down to the quarters for nursing. Delia had her baby. A boy."

"I do not want him nursed by a Negro."

"Now, Mama, isn't it time you were treated like a lady? Most planters' wives don't nurse their own children."

She pushed me away. "Don't tell me what most planters' wives do. Bring me my baby!"

"Of course, Mama. Just take some nice tea first, and this powder the doctor left you. You'll feel better in no time."

"You think I don't know what that doctor and Pegg are doing to me? I won't take it! I want my baby!" She pushed me aside even more forcefully and ran from the room. I ran after her.

"Mama, Mama, come back," I begged.

Out the back door I followed her ethereal form, with her hair flying and her blue silk sacque billowing out behind her. Behind me, Anne and William and Mr. Chitwell came out of the parlor, all calling her. From the corner of my eye I saw Betsy, who'd been playing with Pegg's Letty, drop her doll and stare as her mother flew by.

This was just what Pa didn't want the children to see.

"Patsy! What's wrong?"

Thank God. It was MyJohn and John behind me. I pointed in the direction of the quarters. Mama was just reaching the lane that ran through the cabins. MyJohn gave chase, and I stood watching, leaning against my brother.

At Delia's doorstep MyJohn gathered Mama in his arms and they went inside.

———

" 'TIS A SHAME about the flood," Mama said. The laudanum had quieted her. Edward was sleeping in my arms.

"Flood?" I asked.

"They are saying that it is the worst flood we've ever had. Mr. Jefferson lost his mill on the Rivanna River. And the James and Rappahannock overflowed. Such losses! Four thousand hogsheads of tobacco, crops, livestock, lives, and homes. Oh, the people will go into debt."

"Mama, there was no flood," I said.

She shook her head and sighed. "The people are suffering. And the new governor rides about in a coach given to him by King George."

We didn't have a new governor yet. Governor Boutetourt had died last fall and England had not yet appointed another.

I sat rocking Edward. But oh, my mind was so sullied now with fear! And then guilt. Because the fear was not for Mama. It was for myself.

———

I SETTLED MAMA for a nap and put Edward to sleep in the downstairs cradle. By late afternoon I discovered that Anne and William couldn't be found.

"I haven't seen them," MyJohn said when I called be-lowstairs. Both he and my brother came up.

Little Betsy, who was just learning to put words to-gether, tugged at MyJohn's breeches. "Mill, mill. I wanna go, too."

"So they're at the mill," I said.

"We'll go and fetch them back," MyJohn offered. The mill was a mile away on the river. Both children knew not to go near the water.

"They like to visit the miller and his wife," I said.

"You ought to rest before supper," MyJohn said. "You look spent." He put his arm around my shoulder. "Won't you?"

I pulled away.

"What is it, Patsy?" He peered into my face. His earnest brown eyes were so perplexed, his concern so dear.

"Nothing. I'm worried about Mama."

"Don't worry. We're making her a pleasant retreat downstairs. Patsy, what is it?"

"Oh, MyJohn, I'm afraid." And I commenced to cry.

"What are you afraid of?"

Out of the corner of my eyes I saw my brother John go out the back door, to give us privacy. "Of you," I said.

"Of me?" He made as if to laugh but did not.

"Of what marriage to you will do to me. Of becom-ing like Mama if we wed."

He smiled. "Patsy, darling, of course you might think that, but by heaven, you are the most sensible and steady young woman I have ever known."

"How do we know?" I whispered. "Mama was beautiful and strong, too, when she wed Pa."

MyJohn hesitated for a moment. "How do we know about anything, dearest? There is no promise written in stone that tomorrow won't bring any manner of trouble. Should we deny ourselves happiness in anticipation of it?"

"No."

"Patsy," he said gently, "I greatly esteem your father. But he casts a long shadow. I do not."

"You're saying it's Pa's fault?"

"It's no one's fault. It's just that another woman might have been able to stand up under his long absences, and his preoccupations."

It was almost what Pa had said. "I'm still afraid. I don't think it's Pa. I just think there's too many barons in Mama's family. And that it's in the blood."

"I refuse to allow anything bad to happen to you. I promise," he said.

I smiled and nodded, as if I believed him. I was supposed to believe him, wasn't I? But I would not let him hold me. It was not he who had to do the promising, after all. It was me. And of a sudden, I couldn't.

———

"MAMA, TELL ME how it was when you first met Pa. Were you very much in love?"

The children were not yet back. I'd brought Mama some tea.

"Your pa was a fine man."

I supposed that if I wanted her to talk any, I'd have to abide by her belief that Pa was dead.

"When did you meet him?" Why had I never asked her these questions before?

"Nobody wanted us to wed. Your pa had no money. We were wed in the parlor at Rural Plains."

"I know, Mama, but did you love him?"

"Guests wore powdered wigs, high stocks, hoop-skirts, and all kinds of furbelows. Silk stockings and silver buckles. Oh, there was feasting and dancing, mint julep and eggnog. The wedding feast lasted several days. Then we went to our honeymoon cottage at Pine Slash, given to me by my own pa. The land was poor, but it was three hundred acres. And six Negroes."

"But, Mama, did you love him?"

Her eyes came alert. "They say a true lady should never admit she loves a man," she said solemnly. "It is not consistent with the perfection of female delicacy."

"'Female delicacy'?"

"For a married woman to declare the full extent of affection for her husband might produce disgust in him."

"Who told you that, Mama?"

"A book. *The Ladies Library.* I was raised on it." She giggled. "I went against its teachings once, and what happened? I got in the increasing way with you. But I've tried to make up for it. Always I cultivated a modest reserve and retiring delicacy."

She made up for begetting me?

"Our wedding feast and dancing went on till morning."

She was talking about the gown she wore when I left the room. She was saying something about blue striped satin and pale blue calamanco shoes.

I HEARD ANNE and William clattering into the house.

"Anne bit the head off a butterfly! Look!"

They stood there, just inside the back door. Anne, William, John, and MyJohn. Anne held the creature in her hand. It was spotted, of a lovely golden tone. And true enough, it had no head.

"Stop making up stories!" I scolded. "And where have you both been? Didn't I tell you to be here for your tutor? I've had to dismiss him again!"

"She bit off its *head*," William insisted. "I'm not making up stories."

"Did you?" I demanded of my sister.

She nodded solemnly. Yes.

"Did you eat it?"

"I spit it out."

I could not believe it. Nor the willfulness with which she admitted it.

"Why? Why would you destroy one of God's beautiful creatures like this?" I was filled then with a sudden fear.

Suppose Anne was of Mama's bent? Mayhap *she* was the one who would inherit the madness.

I must take firm action with her, in spite of what Pa had said. I must not let her run wild and unstructured. I must keep a careful eye to her doings.

She stood unafraid before me. "Because I want a new dress the color of the butterfly. That's what you get if you bite off its head."

MyJohn kissed me lightly. "Go easy," he whispered, "they're confused on account of their mama." Then he and John went back downstairs.

"Who told you this?" I demanded of Anne. "Pegg?"

Her refusal to respond gave me the answer.

"And what do you need a new dress for, pray?"

She retrieved a dirty and crumpled paper from her pocket.

It was from Mrs. Hooper. An invitation. "I am pleased to invite your Anne to the delightful Mr. Onslow's Dancing School, which is held in rotation in the homes of pupils in the Williamsburg area. Each pupil will have an individual lesson. There will be picnics, games, and formal dinners for the occasion. Please send your young William and a servant to accompany Anne."

"Evelyn saw us playing by the river and rode over to deliver it," Anne said. "And Evelyn has a new silk dress, the color of a red bird, and she's no older than I am."

I breathed a sigh. "You want to go to this dancing school?"

"It would be great sport."

Her wanting this surprised me. "What about William?" I asked.

"He said he'd sooner be tarred and feathered."

"He'll go with you. But I cannot. I shall send Silvy. But if I hear that you have acted like a rapscallion, or sullied our good name, I shall punish you, you hear?"

"And what about my dress?"

"I shall stitch one up for you of blue cotton."

"Evelyn's got silk!"

"They import it. They go against the nonimportation agreements."

"Everybody will be wearing silk."

"Everybody's father isn't Patrick Henry. You don't know how lucky you are. Evelyn's father is in debt. Like so many other families in Virginia who insist on growing tobacco. Pa long since gave it up for growing wheat and grains."

"I'll tell them you said that." She was uncontrollable.

"You dare!" I whirled on her. I grabbed her arm hard and shook her. "And you are not to say a word about her niece Sarah and Jonathan Snead. Do you hear?"

"I might as well not even go, if I can't talk."

But she heard. I scared her to death, poor child.

"Can I go and see Mama?" Her voice got plaintive. And her face lost its sharp angles and resumed the round innocence of childish need.

"No, she's resting. We can pay her a visit later. Go clean up. Then to the books. I must see to Edward."

Chapter Eight

———

"THE ROOM FOR your mother is finished, love,"
MyJohn said. "Why don't you come down and
see it?"

It was two days later. I was reading the *Gazette*.

*Whereas Martha Beasley, my wife, has absented
herself from me and goes about scandalizing my
character and threatening that she or some of her
associates will swear away my life; and as I am of
the opinion that she has lost her senses: These are
therefore to forward all persons from harboring or
trusting her on my account, for I will not pay any
debt she shall contract, from the date hereof.
Signed, William Beasley.*

"Patsy?"
I read the words over and over. Then I dropped the
paper and picked up the dress I was making for Anne.

"I'm studying on whether to put some lace at the sleeves of Anne's gown. What do you think? She'll likely be the only little girl there without it."

"You must abide by your pa's resolutions," MyJohn said.

"Anne hates it that Pa won't let her wear silk."

"At her age hate comes easily. And doesn't last. What were you reading in the paper?"

"I was just realizing how many notices there are about women running off from their husbands. Mayhap if Mama had run off, you wouldn't have to be building a room for her now."

"Patsy, don't," he pleaded.

"I'm just saying that with these women, running off might be to save their sanity."

"The room is ready for your mama," he said again.

Why is it that when men don't wish to face something they wash it over and pretend it does not exist? I looked down at my stitching.

"You and I are responsible for the younger children," he reminded me. "This is the only way, Patsy."

"I'll be along in a minute," I said.

I'D ALWAYS KNOWN the ceiling was low, but why did it seem so much lower now?

"Pegg put up the curtains," MyJohn offered. He was trying so hard to please me.

They were homespun. And all the hammering I'd heard had been for the new heart-pine floor, which was now covered with animal skins. The wide hearth had always been there, of course. But now a brass kettle hung on a polished crane. There was a heavy oak table. The walls gleamed with whiteness. There was one of Mama's favorite rocking chairs, a clothespress, and a bed with one of her favorite quilts on it.

John and MyJohn stood looking at me, waiting.

"It's beautiful."

"She can come down this very day," MyJohn said.

"Not yet, MyJohn," I said. "She's been quiet and good. Not yet. She needs more time."

"You mean you do."

"All right, yes. I do. I have to become accustomed to this."

He sighed. "I suppose it is accorded to man born of woman to wait," he said.

"Don't blaspheme," I told him. When everything about the whole business was a blasphemy, anyway.

OVER THE NEXT two days I readied clothes for Anne and William to go to the Hoopers'.

And still Mama did not go to the cellar.

MyJohn was patient with me. He waited.

I told him it was better to do it when the children were away. John would see them to the Hoopers' safely. Into a basket I put preserved jellies, pickles, and some pastries. One did not arrive to be a guest at a plantation without bringing along gifts.

Into Anne and William I put the fear of God.

For two days I lectured them on manners. Still, when the chaise drove off, with Silvy sitting between them, Barley driving, and John riding alongside, I had more fears than a cat with a long tail in a room full of rocking chairs.

I should have gone with them, I thought. I shouldn't have allowed Anne to take her lacquered box in which she kept her treasures. That alone could cause trouble with the other girls. Then MyJohn came up behind me. "Good, you got them off," he said. "It's starting to rain."

As I turned to go back inside the house, I saw a white pigeon on the roof.

———

BY THE TIME MyJohn was ready to leave that evening, the rain was steady and vicious. He didn't want to go until John returned. John had been away all afternoon, likely at Dorothea's.

We stood under the covered walkway out back. We were alone, and MyJohn looked as if he wanted to kiss me. But I gave him no encouragement.

"Patsy, you've got to stop this," he said.

"What?"

"You know. We're betrothed. Why won't you kiss me?"

I had no answer. I wanted to. The nearness of him, the manly smells of him, the dear familiar arms and hands, the broad shoulders made me half daft with wanting. Did he think it was easy for me?

I let him kiss me. I huddled in his arms, letting him protect me, until we saw John and Barley ride up.

Both were already soaked through. Barley took the horse and chaise into the barn. MyJohn squeezed my hand and went to speak to my brother. Then he rode off.

John and Barley came in about ten. I gave them supper in the traveler's room. Rain slashed against the windows and pinged into rain barrels. When they'd come in, I'd seen through the open door pools of standing water in the back quadrant. And heard water rushing in rivulets in the lane between the slave houses.

"I'm afraid we're in for the worst of it," John said. "Some people at the Hoopers' said the James and Rappahannock are already threatening to flood."

I thought of Mama. And her predictions. But I said nothing.

John and Barley ate in companionable silence. There was something between these two. They'd grown up together, played together. But, while John still retained some of his boyhood friendship with Barley, it had long since taken on a different tone. Barley was a good hand with the horses John was raising for racing. But John was definitely the master now in the friendship.

Men do this better than women, I decided. Just then there was a tremendous clap of thunder. And I jumped. John got up and set his plate down. "You'd best get to your bed," he advised Barley. "Unless you want to bed down in here for the night."

The fire looked inviting. Barley grinned sheepishly. "You got a quilt, I'd just as soon stay in here if'n it's arright," he said.

So a quilt was fetched. Candles were extinguished. John bolted the outside door and the door from the traveler's room to the house, and saw me to my room. It was a comfort to know John was there.

Outside the rain poured down as if the world were coming to an end. I could not sleep for the sound of it.

———

I MUST HAVE slept, after all, though always my mind was conscious of the terrible rain. The wheat crop will be ruined, I thought. The peach orchard brought down. Then I heard a sound, a thump from outside my window. I got up to peer outside, but I could see nothing in the drenching rain.

Then, in a flash of lightning, I saw it.

Under the linden tree by the white fence! A figure, bedraggled and plodding against the rain.

Mama! I was sure of it! My heart leapt inside me. And in her arms she held something. A child?

I ran to Edward's cradle on the other side of my bed. He lay sleeping peacefully. Who, then?

Betsy!

I ran out into the hall and down to her room. Betsy's bed was empty.

"John? John!" I pounded on his door. "John, wake up!"

"What is it, Patsy? What's amiss?" He stood there, half asleep.

"John, I just saw Mama outside! Carrying Betsy!"

———

JOHN TUGGED BREECHES over his nightshirt, put on a hunting shirt, and took up a lantern. Then he went to the traveler's room to wake Barley. I somehow got dressed, though my hands were trembling.

"Everyone, get lanterns," John directed. We stood in the dogtrot between the kitchen and the house. "Patsy, put a shawl around yourself. Barley, get the horses. And a rope. Pegg, wake the other servants and Mr. Melton."

In minutes John had consulted with Mr. Melton and mounted his own bay gelding. "Barley, you come with me," John ordered. "Mr. Melton will take another search group. Patsy, stay in the house, else you'll take cold. You and Pegg keep a lookout, in case she comes back." And they went off into the howling darkness.

"It's my fault, Pegg," I said. We stood under the outside walkway, watching the dark figures disappear between the dependencies and the barn. "I refused to put her in the cellar room. I couldn't do it. Now, if something happens to Betsy, it will be my fault."

She made a low, sympathetic sound in her throat but did not disavow what I said. "I'm gonna go inside an' put up some coffee for those mens," she told me. "They be in need of somethin' hot when they get back. Wish Silvy was here. Alice, you come and help. We get out some ham and biscuits. Patsy, that chile gonna need dry things when she gets back."

"I'll get them. And some for Mama. And John." I moved along the covered walkway, never taking my eyes from the dark.

IT TOOK TWO hours for them to find Mama and Betsy. When John did hear the child cry out in answer to his hoarse voice, it was from the confines of an old shed near the mill by the New Found River. He came home with Betsy on the saddle in front of him. She was wrapped in his hunting shirt and a blanket he'd taken along, with his tricorn on her head. Water plastered John's hair down and ran from his face and body.

Mama was on Barley's horse, her wrists tied to the saddle with the rope, Barley leading it.

"Oh, thank God!" I made John go and change, ordered Alice to feed all the servants who had taken part in the search, and took the soaked, sobbing, and frightened Betsy to her chamber to strip off her sodden nightdress, dry her hair, and give her a bit of rum to warm her.

"Mama say we run away an' find Anne and Will."

I looked up at Pegg. She had just returned from seeing that Mama was warm and dry in her room. For some reason, of late, Mama had changed her mind about Pegg trying to poison her.

"She say you send Will and Anne away," Pegg reported quietly. "An' you not gonna get Betsy."

"Dear God! Preserve us." I was weeping and hugging Betsy so close she could scarce breathe.

In the traveler's room, I saw to John and Barley.

"I've tied Mama to her bed," John told me.

In the fire's flickering light he looked like Pa standing there, tall and somber. Pa had always had that look about him, of being a little bit besieged. And haunted.

We're all haunted, I thought.

"In the morning, Patsy," John said. "In the morning."

He should never have had to tie Mama to her bed. I know how much he loved her. And what it must have cost him to do so.

"I know, John," I answered. "In the morning she goes into the cellar."

Chapter Nine

Whereas: Anne Murphey, wife of James Murphey, hath in a clandestine manner left his Plantation in Prince William County, about 7 o'clock this morning, and hath taken up her residence elsewhere. She has fettered the tender cords that tied her family's souls together: This is to forewarn all Persons from entertaining or dealing with her for I will not pay any Debts which she shall contract from the date hereof. —James Murphey

I READ THAT the next morning at breakfast. And I hoped that Anne Murphey had found some people to entertain and deal with her.

IT WAS STILL raining heavily. When he came into the dining room and poured himself some coffee, MyJohn reported ruined fields, roads of mud knee-deep, and carriages mired in them. He'd seen broken fences, livestock wandering, and water pouring forth in places it had no right to be.

"How is your family's place?" I asked.

"Well, you know we're on a hill, though we've got ruined crops, too."

"You should have stayed."

"Patsy, I was frantic over you. I heard that someone tried to kidnap Betsy."

My heart thudded inside me. "Where did you hear that?"

"Everyone I met on the road here. Of course, the servants reassured me once I arrived. How is she?"

"Still sleeping. I was up with her most of the night."

"Where did you find them?" he asked John.

"An old shed near the mill at the river."

"God's shoe buckles!" He was struck silent by the whole thing. "Well, you've done your pa proud," he told John. And then to me. "We know what we must do now."

I decided that I could write my own notice for the *Gazette. Whereas: Sarah Henry hath tried to drown one of her children, and ran off in the middle of the night in a storm with another, her family has decided, with all convenient speed, to confine her to the cellar in her home. She has fettered the tender cords that tied their souls together, and has, from some time past, tried to ruin them. This is to forewarn all persons from dealing with her, for we, her family, are parted in affection.*

"Since we can't expect your tutor this morning, John,

why don't you see if David needs help?" MyJohn suggested.

"I can stay and help you," John said. "In case there's trouble with Mama."

"I know you can," MyJohn told him. "But there won't be trouble, and David will need you more."

John went. On the way out of the room he passed my chair, and I grabbed his hand and held it. Just for an instant.

———

As WE WENT to Mama's chamber to fetch her, Delia presented herself at the house. "I'se come for his midmorning feeding, Miss."

I looked at her in vexation, then softened. She was small and gentle, less than a week out of childbed, and openly fearful of being in the big house. You would think she was reporting at the gates of heaven itself.

"Come along," I said.

But when Mama saw her, she became anxious. "She's going to steal my baby," she said.

Pegg had brought Edward into the room.

"Delia's going to nurse Edward, Mama," I said gently.

Instantly she ran to Pegg and snatched the baby away. "Nobody's going to care for my child but me! You hear, Patsy? You think I'm not sensible of what you are trying to do? Take him from me, is what. All of you are!"

She stood there clutching little Edward so tightly I thought he'd smother.

"We came to show you the new room we made for you downstairs, Aunt Sarah," MyJohn said. He moved toward her, put his hand on her shoulder, and kissed her forehead gently. Then he touched Edward's face. "Growing into the spitting image of his father," he said fondly.

"Yes," Mama said. "Too bad Patrick didn't live to see him born."

"Yes," MyJohn agreed. "Too bad." He told Mama she could take baby Edward with us when we looked at the new room. He spoke in lulling tones as he led her.

Please God, I prayed, don't let her drop Edward. Please let us get her downstairs safely.

MyJohn talked her all the way down. In the room, which was lighted by a profusion of candles because of the dank morning, Mama looked around.

"This is pretty," she said. "I shall come down here when I wish to have some moments of peace."

"Of course," MyJohn told her. "It's why we made it for you." Then he motioned me away, back up the stairs.

"Here, look at the hearth. You can even cook your wonderful desserts down here. Let me hold the baby."

She gave little Edward over to him.

Again MyJohn motioned me out of the room.

The last I saw, Mama was examining the skillets and pans on the hearth. And John was handing Edward over to Pegg, who came quickly to the stairs and motioned me up.

On the ground floor we closed the door behind us, and I handed Edward to Delia, who was waiting in the hall.

Within minutes I heard the screaming.

I heard things being thrown. Heard MyJohn's voice saying, "Don't, Aunt Sarah." And then, "Oh!"

I leaned with my head against the door to the cellar. It was Pegg who pulled me away as Mama's screams echoed belowstairs.

"Give me my baby! What do you mean I must stay down here! Patsy! Patsy! Come help me! Patsy, please!"

The door opened. I did not see, because Pegg would not allow me to look, but I could hear Mama on the stairs, struggling with MyJohn.

And when he came up and the door closed behind him with a thud, I saw that his shirt was torn. His hair was mussed. His stock was untied. There were scratches on his face and a bruise, red and already starting to swell, on his cheekbone.

Belowstairs Mama was still screaming, but the door and the floors were thick. You could scarce hear it unless you knew to listen for the sound. I went weak and knelt on the floor in the hall and put my hands over my ears. But the sound tore at my heart. "Patsy! Patsy!"

Why me? Why not John or MyJohn? I knew I would hear that scream for the rest of my life.

———

I TOOK MYSELF out of the house all that afternoon. The rain still fell, but I went to the barn and saddled Jolly, my horse. Then I rode along my favorite paths, to my favorite haunts, in spite of the pouring rain.

It felt good on my face. I became soaked through, but

that felt good, too. I came back after an hour of riding only because I feared that Jolly would stumble in the soggy ground. In the barn I rubbed her down instead of letting Barley do it. After changing, I stayed in the detached kitchen, baking. Betsy, just out of bed, played quietly on the floor near me. Pegg, who had a way with a needle and thread, had made her a new rag doll.

Once, Betsy tugged at my skirt. I looked down. "Mama?" she asked.

"Mama is resting," I said. "She's sickly and needs her rest."

It worked for the moment. But I wondered how long the younger ones would be content with such an answer.

———

I DON'T KNOW how I would have survived the day if Clementina Rind hadn't stopped by to call.

The wheels of her chaise were mud covered, as was the horse pulling it.

"How did you get through?" I asked. "Isn't most everything flooded out?"

"I started out yesterday to see how the locals were faring in the heavy rain, so I could write a story. Stayed the night with my sister. Then I decided to come and see you." She stood on the front stoop, wet through, taking off her buckled shoes and striped stockings.

Barley, who'd seen her driving up the road, took her horse and chaise to the barn, and I invited her inside.

"You'd best stay the night. It'll be supper time soon. And I can't let you start back to Williamsburg. You'll never get through with the chaise. And I can't let you chance those roads."

"I've a story to write," she said.

"You can write it here. We'll have one of the servants take it to town for you."

"Thank you."

"What have you heard of the storm? How are our neighbors faring?"

"Around here, just ruined crops and orchards. But we hear in town that it's worse on the Rivanna and James Rivers. Cattle have been lost, houses washed away. Thomas Jefferson lost his mill."

It was as if a thunderbolt hit me then. We were in the hall, and I stopped in my tracks. "Oh, no!"

"What is it, Patsy?"

"My mama said that would happen. She said the flood would happen, too. Can it be possible, Clementina? Pegg says she has the sight."

"It could be just coincidence."

"And you know what she said about your husband," I reminded her.

"Yes." She looked uncomfortable. Worried of a sudden. So I dropped the subject and we went inside. I brought her to my chamber and got some dry clothing for her. We were about the same size. I sat on my bed while she changed.

"I've been paying mind to all the notices in the paper about runaway wives," I told her.

"What's troubling you, Patsy?" She tied a fresh apron around her waist.

"I just wondered if maybe Mama should have run off. If maybe she'd be all right now if she had."

Clementina tucked her hair under a dry mobcap. "Your mama is not the kind to do such. You're melancholy, aren't you? Where are the children?"

"Attending dancing school at the Hoopers'."

She put a hand on my shoulder. "Come make me a cup of coffee. And you can tell me what you know of the dancing school at the Hoopers'."

———

THE RAIN GOT even heavier. We took our coffee in the front parlor. I brought baby Edward in and held him on my lap. The darling behaved so that he made me proud.

Once, during our conversation, there came a faint thump from belowstairs.

We exchanged looks. "Clementina, how am I to abide this?" I whispered. "It's like there's an animal confined down there."

"You must think of this little fellow," she said. And she reached across the round table to take his hand. Edward grasped her finger.

"Yes. You are right." I hugged Edward close. His sturdy little body comforted me. His coos and gurgles guided my reason.

"Did I tell you? I'm going to run a poetry contest for women," Clementina said. "You'd be surprised how many hereabouts put pen to paper. You write poetry, Patsy. You must write a poem for the contest."

I looked at her serene face. Write a poem? About

what? Then I heard a thump from the cellar. About my mother in the cellar, I thought.

I smiled back and said mayhap I would.

THE MORE I THOUGHT about it, the more I knew what I must do.

Mama had the sight. No amount of shilly-shallying around the subject could deny that. Not with the storm and flood outside.

After supper, when the children were quiet and I'd put an exhausted Clementina in Mama's old room, I went into the kitchen. "Put up a plate of food and I'll bring it down to Mama," I told Pegg.

"You oughtn't to do that, Miss Patsy," she said.

"Well," I snapped, "do any of you want to do it?"

Nobody answered. "She been quiet," Pegg said. "Maybe we should leave her be."

"And maybe we should leave her to starve," I said. "Fix the plate, and bring it to me." I felt like the mistress of the household. It was a good feeling, and I hoped it would last.

Chapter Ten

SHE SAT ON A BENCH by the hearth, holding a cake mold in her hands. The fire was near out. The room was chilled.

On the floor at her feet there was flour and some broken eggs.

"Mama? Mama, I have supper for you."

For a moment there was no recognition in her eyes. The front of her chemise and petticoat were stained. Her mobcap was off, and there was flour in her hair, which was in the most pitiable arrangement I have ever seen.

"How can I make this cake when I have no frogs' legs?" she asked me.

"Mama, you don't need frogs' legs."

"What do you know about cooking? All the best cakes have frogs' legs."

I gave her the food I'd brought. She ate. Tears kept coming out of my eyes while I watched her. "Mama, it rained like you said it would. We have terrible floods. I think you have the sight. You can tell what's going to happen. And I need to know some things."

She smiled.

"Who is going to inherit what you have, Mama? Which of us girls? Will it be me? Or Anne? Or Betsy?"

She leaned closer to me. "The frogs' legs, if cut up properly, make just the right spice for a cake," she said.

I left her there with her food and went back upstairs.

THE FIRST THING I saw when Anne, William, and Silvy returned after a week away was that Anne had cut her hair. Short. It came just below her ears.

"What did you do?"

She stood next to the Hooper chaise, sassy as ever. "The other girls wanted to see how I'd look if my hair was short." She shook her head. The hair bounced. "I like it." She grinned.

"You look like a boy!"

"Now I can be a pirate. Like Anne Bonny and sail with Captain Calico Rackman."

"How could you do that to your hair!"

"Or maybe I'll be like Mad Ann Baily. She dressed in buckskins, carried a tomahawk, and collected Indian scalps. And she came to Virginia in 1750 as an indentured servant!"

"Know what I learned?" from William.

I sent the driver of the chaise to the kitchen for some repast and walked the children to the house. "What?"

"I learned what part of the swine's foot the devil resides in."

"God's shoe buckles!" I stopped on the path to the house. "Pa says this is the age of oratory, the age of enlightened men! And you two are going back to witchery and piracy! Was there no civility at the Hoopers'? No dancing?"

They looked shamefaced. "We danced," William said. "Know what they're saying at the Hoopers'?"

"Dare I ask?"

"That there's a crazy woman in the cellar at Scotchtown."

Dear God!

But I mustn't let them see my concern. "Oh, Mrs. Hooper's just in a pet because their name was published in the *Gazette* for going against the nonimportation laws," I told them.

Anne giggled. "Guess who we met in the woods on the way home? Sarah Hallam and Jonathan Snead."

"What do you mean 'in the woods'?"

"Just that," Anne said excitedly. "They had horses. When she ran off, Sarah took a horse and Jonathan had his. And they're living in the woods. Like Indians!"

"And they're happy," William said.

"And they're not married. But they're going to be, soon's they find a preacher," said Anne.

"Aren't they terribly wet from the storm?" I asked.

"Oh yes," Anne said. "They said they'd been soaked and were looking for shelter. I invited them here."

"You what?"

"Well"—she looked up at me—"doesn't Pa always say we should open our doors to those less fortunate than us?"

I said nothing. She was right.

"Where's Mama?" she asked.

"We want to see her," William said.

I looked down at their upturned faces. "She's resting."

"She's the crazy woman in the cellar, isn't she?" Anne asked.

"No. She isn't crazy."

"Then we want to see her," William said firmly.

"Even if she is crazy, we want to see her," Anne put in.

Their eyes were swords, piercing me. I don't know what I would have done if Pegg hadn't come into the room just then.

"Miss Patsy, Betsy wet the bed last night."

"Betsy doesn't wet at night anymore," I said.

Pegg grunted. "She do now." And her eyes met mine, almost defiantly.

Anne whispered to me. "You ought to let Pegg help Mama, with her remedies. She's the seventh daughter of a seventh daughter, and they have powers."

Oh God, I thought, how am I to tell them about Mama? What am I to tell them? They shouldn't see her as she is now. But how to keep them from seeing her?

I glanced helplessly at Pegg. She shooed the children from the room. "Miss Patsy, what you gonna do 'bout the children?"

"What's to be done?" I asked dismally.

"I fancy the reason Betsy be startin' to wet is 'cause she wanna go back to bein' a baby. To the way it was then, when her mama weren't crazy."

"You fancy that, do you?"

"Yes." She stood before me, taller because of the turban she wore. Rings dangling from her ears. She was very tall and her carriage was excellent. She was not beautiful, as white people describe beauty, but she was in another way. In the way that her eyes spoke, and her mouth held firm. And in the pride that I could never have.

If that was not beauty, what was?

"An' Anne can't go back to wettin' the bed. So she gonna give you trouble in other ways. Only way she can think of now is to cut her hair. And William. The other day I see him in the barn wif one of Mr. MyJohn's pipes. Smokin'."

I sighed.

"All the children in a state on account of your mama. You gotta tell them the truth about her."

"I have no truth to tell," I snapped. "What truth is there?"

"There be only one truth, Miss Patsy. An' if you can't do it, I will. I can, but you gots to give me back the authority I always had round heah, Miss Patsy."

"I never told the children you didn't have authority."

"They knows it. By the way you talk to me. You always tellin' Anne not to mind my stories."

"I'm mistress of the place now. Pa wants it that way." It was all I could think of to say.

"Well, of course you is, Miss Patsy!" Her tone was smooth as honey. "But you gots to give me authority with the children, else they don't listen and run wild."

Oh, it would be so easy to do as she wanted. But I would be giving in to her. Handing back the reins.

"You is tired," she said. "How long has it been since you worked on your linens for your dowry chest?"

The chest sat in a corner of the room, closed. It was a handsome piece of furniture. John had made it for me two years ago. I sighed. "I've been busy," I said.

"You always passed happy hours with that sewing," she reminded me.

I did not want to be reminded. "To what end? I may decide not to wed, anyway."

Her eyes went wide. "You not gonna marry that dear man who's out there knee-high in mud in your father's fields? Miss Patsy, is you feverish?"

"It's my business if I wed or not. Why should I? So I can end up like Mama?"

The yellow brown eyes lighted with understanding. She picked up some pillows from the settee and put them behind my head. She lighted the hearth and brought over a crewelwork footstool. She took off my shoes and put my feet on the stool. "You jus' need rest. Then your mind will clear. Didn't Pegg always take care of you?"

She was kneeling by the footstool. She started to rub my feet. "You depend on Pegg. On all of us. You all can't run this place without the Negroes, Miss Patsy. Your pa knows that."

I said nothing.

"You give me permission to tell the children the truth about their mama. An' I'll make it right with them. You be surprised at how much children understand."

She wanted her authority back. For this she would return the favor by taking the children in hand and explaining to them about Mama.

Whereas, I thought, I am tired and confused, and don't know what to do about Betsy wetting the bed, and Anne cutting her hair, and Will smoking, I am obliged to make use of this method to bring the household back to order.

"Are you the seventh daughter of a seventh daughter?" I asked.

She lowered her eyes. "Yes."

"I don't believe in that hogwash, but yes, if you can explain to the children about Mama, I would be beholden to you."

Chapter Eleven

THAT NIGHT, ANNE SLIPPED into my room and bed, when all the house was quiet. It had been a long time since she had so sought me out.

"To what do I owe the honor?" I asked.

"Don't scold, Patsy. All you do is scold these days. You're getting to be an old hen."

"Old hens often take chicks under their wings. Did you like it at the Hoopers'?"

"No. Mrs. Hooper is a frightful bore. All she talks about is her family name. And how she did for her niece Sarah, and now Sarah ran off with a savage. Is Jonathan Snead really a savage? He didn't look like one to me."

"He was adopted by a family in Williamsburg when he was a boy. And he went to the Brafferton School for Indians at the college. He's part Catawba. But he acquitted himself well in school and is to be an interpreter between colonial authorities and his tribe."

"Then why doesn't he let his tribe marry them?"

"I suppose it's Sarah. Mayhap she wants a Christian wedding."

"I'd like to run off with an Indian."

"I'm sure you would."

"What are you reading?"

"A book Mama said she was raised on. I want to see what she learned."

"Read some to me."

And so I did. "'Be careful in displaying your good sense. It will be thought you assume a superiority over the rest of the company.'"

"I don't understand," Anne said. "Isn't that what Pa is always telling us to have? Good sense?"

I sighed. "Yes."

"Read more."

I did. "'Wit is the most dangerous talent a girl can possess.'" We giggled over that. And over the maxim that "love is never to begin on the woman's part."

Anne looked up at me. "Pegg told me and Will about Mama," she said.

I closed the book. "What did she tell?"

"That Mama's mind is in some other place. Someplace we can't go. And how she has the sight. And that's why we must leave her downstairs, so she can write down what is to come. But that we must leave her in peace."

"Yes, that's the right of it," I said.

"Could I visit her once in a while?"

"No. I don't think so. I think she must really have peace and quiet."

She nodded and snuggled closer to me, and for a while we captured again the old sisterly affection that I had long since thought was gone.

————

THE NEXT MORNING while we were at breakfast, Pegg came into the dining room. "Miss Patsy, there's people at the front door." Then she looked at MyJohn. "That Sarah girl. The one what's run off from the Hoopers'. And the man she wif. They look to be in a bad way, Miss Patsy."

Anne jumped up. "I knew she'd come."

"Sit," I snapped.

She obeyed. "I'll see to it," MyJohn said. I went with him.

————

SARAH HALLAM WAS TALL and strongly built, with fine teeth, and hair the color of straw, and eyes so blue as to bewitch you. I envied her the fine jawline, the beautiful skin, and perfect nose. I envied her strength as she stood in our hallway that morning.

She was soaked through and shivering. Her skirt was muddy, her hair darkened with rainwater, her face drawn.

Behind her was Jonathan Snead, looking as handsome as ever, but sheepish and wet.

"Hello, you two. Come in!" MyJohn said. "Terrible weather." He sounded so hearty. As if we welcomed sought-after runaways to our door every day of the week.

"Don't you know the whole county's been looking for you?" I asked.

"We do," Sarah said. "Which is why we have hidden. Last night we took refuge in your barn. We hope you don't mind."

"Barn! Why didn't you come to the door?" asked MyJohn. "Mr. Henry would take on something terrible if he knew you stayed in the barn."

"If you're part Indian," Anne said to Jonathan, "why couldn't you make a lean-to in the woods and keep dry?"

"Anne!" I said sharply. "I told you to stay in the dining room." Then to Jonathan, "I'm sorry."

He smiled, showing beautiful white teeth. "So am I. Not that she said it, but because she's right. I've been too long away from my people," he told Anne. "I've lost the old ways."

———

I ARRANGED FOR Sarah to have a change of clothing, and MyJohn looked after Jonathan. Then we gave them breakfast.

They could scarce keep from holding hands at the table. Anne's eyes were bulging out of her head, watching them.

"We don't wish to make trouble for you all with your neighbors," Jonathan said, as he devoured the food. "Especially with Mrs. Hooper."

"There's not much we have to do to make trouble with the Hoopers," I assured them.

They told us how they'd been living, traveling from town to town, trying to get a minister to marry them.

"But all had seen the notice in the *Gazette*," Jonathan said, "and bade me take Sarah back home."

She laughed. "My aunt wouldn't take me back now. I'm a ruined woman." And she clasped Jonathan's hand on the table.

"Are you really ruined?" Anne asked. I could tell she was delighted with the idea.

I shushed her.

"Is it because you got your clothes all wet?" she pushed. "Like happened to my doll one time when I left her out in the rain?"

Sarah smiled. "Yes, just like that, Anne," she said.

"Patsy," Anne looked at me. "Can't we give Sarah some new clothes so she isn't ruined anymore?"

I said yes, we could.

"Then we lost our horses," Jonathan went on. "They got away and likely went back to the Hoopers. Which I suppose my people would dishonor me for. And we've no place else to go, so we came here. We know your pa for a good man, Patsy."

"You're welcome to our hospitality," MyJohn said. "Mr. Henry is away, but he's due home soon."

"What we were thinking," Jonathan said slowly, "was that since your pa knows so many people, he could maybe persuade a minister to marry us."

I buttered some bread. "You both just make yourselves to home until you can ask him."

———

OF COURSE, WHEN Pa arrived home that evening, he went right to helping Sarah and Jonathan. He was scarce out of his wet cloak and muddy boots, but he sent a servant with a letter to his uncle, Reverend Henry, rector of St. Paul's.

"We'll have the wedding here, Patsy. In our parlor. Find a suitable gown for Sarah. Have Pegg and Silvy make up a wedding feast."

William pulled on Pa's sleeve. "Tell us about the flood," he begged.

He did so, at supper. "The James rose sixteen inches in one hour. On the Rappahannock, houses floated with the currents. People were on makeshift rafts and shouting for help. Wine casks, furniture, hogsheads of tobacco all floated away in the waters."

Betsy and William were openmouthed.

But Anne never took her eyes from Sarah and Jonathan.

After supper Pa slipped downstairs to see Mama. And when he came back up, I thought how pale he looked, how broken. But still, he played his violin for us in the front parlor. Handel and Vivaldi. Mama's favorites. As well as country tunes.

He told Sarah and Jonathan he was playing for them, but as I watched him I knew he was playing for Mama.

There were tears in his eyes.

"My pa taught himself to play when he was twelve," Anne whispered to Sarah. "He broke his collarbone and had nothing else to keep him busy."

Sarah whispered something back, but I couldn't hear it.

"He can play the lute and harpsichord, too," Anne boasted.

Pa could stay only two days. Then he had to attend an

emergency session of the House of Burgesses, to help decide what to do about the great spring flood in the Tidewater and Piedmont regions.

———

BECAUSE SHE WAS bigger than I was, the only gown I could find for Sarah was one of Mama's. Of course, Anne came right along after us as I opened the clothespress.

I showed Sarah all Mama's dresses and petticoats.

"Oh, I couldn't," she said.

"You can and you will. I want you to," I said.

She was happy with a sprigged muslin. But I gave her more to take with her: a striped petticoat, two clean chemises, two mobcaps, two crisp white aprons, a summer cloak, and stockings.

Then I brought her to my room, to my dowry chest, and gave her a set of clean, pressed linens. "Take them. I may not wed after all."

"Patsy! Why would you say such? Anyone can see how smitten MyJohn is with you."

I shook my head and looked at the floor, under which I thought I heard some voices. "There's your answer, down below," I said. "I don't want to come to such an end."

"Why should you? Patsy, I've seen your sadness. You're no longer the sprightly miss I met at all those assemblies."

"My mama's mad," I said. "And I fear that having her blood in my veins the same will happen to me."

"Might be you have your pa's blood?"

"No, it's a woman's malady." I looked at her. "Aren't you afraid of what marriage will bring?"

Her smile was serene. "No. We will face the challenges together."

"Oh, Sarah, how I esteem you! I'm so afraid."

We hugged. I envied her so, with her sureness and her love. And then I showed her the silk gown I had made for myself, which I'd showed no one.

"Shall you wear it?" she asked.

"I don't know," I said shyly. "It stands for something now that I don't quite understand. I won't, until after I wed. If I do. So then, in wearing it, I suppose I'd go against both Mama and Pa. I suppose that's what it stands for."

———

ANNOUNCEMENT IN THE *Virginia Gazette*:

> *Married: Two evenings past, at Scotchtown, the home of Mr. Patrick Henry, Jr., Miss Sarah Hallam, niece of Mr. and Mrs. Hooper of Hooper Run Plantation in Hanover County, and Mr. Jonathan Snead of this town. The mutual affection and similarity of disposition in this agreeable pair afford the strongest assurance of their enjoying the highest felicity in the nuptial state.*

I helped write the announcement. Pa had called himself Patrick Henry, Jr., because that's the way he signed his name. It was out of respect for his uncle, the Reverend Patrick Henry, for whom he was named.

———

As REVEREND HENRY said the words over Sarah and Jonathan, I watched Pa's face. His head was down, so I couldn't see his eyes. What was he thinking?

I knew what I was thinking.

From belowstairs came some thumping. We paid no mind.

Chapter Twelve

———

WE WERE COLLECTING clothing for the flood victims. Pa had sent a note around from the House of Burgesses. John was to get word to all our neighbors.

I was routing around in my brother's room for out-grown breeches when Silvy came to the door. "Miz Patsy? Your sister Anne? She been sneakin' down to see your mama."

Silvy did not always agree with Pegg, and she knew this was wrong enough to tell me. "How?" was all I could think to ask.

She shrugged. "By the door in the hall, Miz Patsy."

"No, I mean how has no one paid mind to this?"

"We been all busy wif the flood, Miz Patsy. YourJohn been gatherin' foodstuffs to send an' we all been helpin'."

"Yes." I sighed and stood up. "Is Anne all right?"

"Right as rain. And she say your mama talkin' sense to her, too."

How could that be? All Mama talked about to me was her wedding day. And needing frogs' legs for a cake.

"Send Anne to me," I said.

———

I TRIED TO recollect what Pa had said about me and Anne. That I must give her a superiority of understanding. There was nothing I felt I owned less of at the moment than understanding. Not even for myself.

"Why did you go to see Mama without permission?" I asked when she came to the door of John's room. "She can get agitated. She might even hurt you. And your presence might send her further inside herself."

She shrugged. "She asked me about the wedding."

"How did she know about the wedding?"

"She heard new voices and heard bustling about more than usual. I told her about it. She was glad for them. I told her you gave Sarah her sprigged muslin."

"She spoke plain to you?" She was lying, I was sure of it.

"We understand each other," she said.

"So she knows Pa's alive, then."

"No. She says he's dead."

"You mustn't go down again, Anne." I made my voice kind. "She could turn on you, as she did on MyJohn and Pa."

"All right," she agreed. "But she said something to me that I should pursue."

I was kneeling on the floor again, my back to her. "What is that?" I asked indifferently.

"She said next time I come down, she'll tell me which of us will inherit her bad blood."

———

THERE WAS SO much work to be done to restore the fields and crops and broken fences from the storm that in the week or so that followed I scarce saw MyJohn.

Which was just as well. Because I knew he wouldn't countenance what I was thinking.

But I could think of nothing else. Was it possible Mama would communicate this to Anne? Was Anne just teasing me, so I'd allow her to go down and talk to Mama again?

For two days I was so taken with learning who would inherit the bad blood, I could think of little else.

And always, in the background, in the shadows, I felt my sister watching me. Was that a smirk on her face?

I had told her I would ponder the matter of her going down to visit Mama again. To my surprise, she did not disobey me and sneak down. She was waiting for my blessing.

Finally, on the third day, I said this to her: "All right, Anne, you may go down and visit Mama. But after MyJohn goes home at night, for he'd never countenance any of this. And John and I will wait at the top of the stairs for you."

"I'm not afraid," Anne said.

"We'll keep watch, anyway." I had confided in John, and he'd agreed. I think only to make me happy.

"Very well," Anne said, "but I want the door closed. If Mama thinks anyone is listening, she won't confide in me."

I wanted to slap her for her smugness, but I didn't.

"You'd best let it lie fallow," Pegg said, having overheard us.

"Why?" I asked.

"No sense in knowin' things you can't do nuthin' about."

"If Mama says it isn't me who will inherit, I'll wed," I told her.

"An' if she says it is you?"

I said nothing. I thought I heard her chuckle, low, when she left the room.

———

THE SERVANTS WERE all in the detached kitchen out back. John and I stood in the hall at the back of the house. That door was open and from outside came the fragrance of lilacs and honeysuckle and what hay had been salvaged.

As promised, John and I closed the door to the cellar, then stood there looking at each other.

"You think I'm wrong, don't you, about letting her go down there?"

John's eyes sought the scene outside the back door. He was looking toward the stables, where his heart lay with his horses. "No. But I think Anne's leading you on a merry chase. And I can't help wondering, Patsy..." His voice wandered off.

"What?"

"Why must you push this?"

"I'm not afraid to know what she says. I must know."

"Suppose it's you, then?"

"I'll not wed."

"Does MyJohn know of this?"

"Of course not, silly." I pushed his arm. "Why do you think I swore you to secrecy? And you mustn't tell him. Either way. Ever! Promise?"

He promised. I knew I could trust him.

"And if it's Anne, then?" he asked.

"She's young enough so I can still mold her, watch her. At least I'll know to look for things. I'm doing this more for her than for myself, John," I said.

We waited. We could hear nothing from downstairs, except quiet. Quiet was good, I decided.

"Are you coming to the steeplechase next week?" he asked.

"Of course! We all are. We want to see you race. And Small Hope win."

John smiled. "Dorothea is coming."

"Oh, wonderful."

"You haven't let Pa know I'm seeing her, have you?"

"Of course not, John. You're not the only one who can keep a still tongue in their head around here, you know."

Moments passed. Eternity passed. I could feel its clock's hands passing over my face, deciding my fate. Outside I could see fireflies. Dusk deepened. "I have to get Will and Betsy in soon," I told John.

Just then we heard footsteps on the stairs on the other

side of the door. We looked at each other. As agreed upon, we waited for Anne's soft knock.

There it was! John opened the door. "Is everything all right?"

But she would not look at him. Or me. She pushed the door open, nearly knocking us down. I saw John take a quick peek down the stairs to see if Mama was pursuing her.

Nobody. He slammed the door shut and locked it. But not before we heard Mama's hysterical laughter.

Anne was gone, out the back door, and toward the quarters. Running as if the devil himself pursued her.

"ANNE."

She had run inside the clapboard house where Pa's law clerks slept. She stood by the window, looking out. I saw her chest heaving. Her fists were clenched. I went to her softly.

"Are you all right, Anne?"

She nodded yes.

"Do you want to tell me what Mama said?"

Tears were in her eyes. Her face, thin and angular rather than pretty, looked years older. She nodded again.

I took her by the hand and led her over to a settle, where we sat down. I waited.

"It won't be you who inherits the bad blood," she said.

"Then, who?"

"Me."

"Oh, Anne!" I tried to hug her, but she wouldn't let me. She pushed me away. "It doesn't matter. I shall never wed. I've already decided that."

"Anne, I shall help you. Together, we'll prepare you so you can push aside this fate. We can make our own fate, you know."

"Like Mama?"

"It doesn't have to be that way, Anne. What about Pa, off all the time helping to make the fate of the country? He isn't just sitting back letting the king have his way, is he? Besides, mayhap she is wrong."

"Like she was wrong about the flood?"

"Anne!"

"Leave me be. Go to MyJohn, why don't you? Now you can wed, don't you see? You and MyJohn can wed."

"How did you know I had such concerns?"

For an instant I saw a smirk of satisfaction. "I was under your bed in your room the day you gave Sarah the clothes. I heard everything."

And with a dignity of manner I did not think she possessed, she walked out the door.

1773

Anne

Chapter Thirteen

February 1773

A NNE, YOU OUGHT to be finished with that broom today. You can't shilly-shally over it much longer."

I was in the detached kitchen, making a broom out of broomcorn. Patsy would have it made out of nothing else. She said brooms were made of it in Italy near two centuries ago. And Benjamin Franklin planted seeds and raised some of the corn. And so did Thomas Jefferson.

"After, you can start the gingerbread."

I'd finish the broom, all right. But afterwards I'd right well get on my horse, Patches, and ride out into the countryside. We could well afford to buy brooms in town, even those made of guinea wheat, made up in Connecticut. But Patsy would hold sway over me.

She'd been doing so, or thought she'd been doing so, for two years now. And I'd been fighting her, bucking her, just like a new calf bucks its mother to get some milk.

Still, she had me doing everything in her effort to keep

me from becoming like Mama. Her goal was to make me a woman of unsullied reputation, a woman who was affable, cheerful, cleanly industrious, and perfectly qualified to direct and manage the female concerns of a plantation.

Maybe, I thought for the thousandth time, I should have made a better lie of it. Maybe I shouldn't have told her I was the one to inherit the bad blood.

Maybe I should have said it was Betsy.

At four, Betsy can almost stitch a hem. And she'd become a solemn little thing, on her way to being a cleanly industrious female already. She follows Patsy around like a hound dog. Don't think it didn't come to me to put the curse on Betsy.

But that would have been taking the easy path. I'm not as all-fired educated as Patsy, but it reasoned to me that Patsy would have worn Betsy right into the ground.

So I said it was me.

I said it because Patsy never would have believed the truth. She would have thought I lied. And it was really her. And then she never would have wed MyJohn. And he's a man of good parts, and smitten with her. And we need him around here to defuse Patsy's harshness.

So I said it was me.

At least I have the mettle to fight back. Although there are times when it does try my spirit. And Pa—don't even think of Pa. Pa, who is so brisk for justice, has never once stepped in to keep Patsy from plaguing me. And that's what hurts most of all.

———

IT HAD SNOWED yesterday, but this morning the snow was gone and the sun as warm as May. MyJohn called it an "aberration of nature." I had to ask him to explain to me what the word meant.

"It means it goes against what is right. It goes against the true nature of things," he said.

Well, I wanted to say, a lot of things around here do. Then I wanted to ask him if keeping Mama in the cellar was an aberration, but I didn't. Because he is such a good person, I couldn't give him sass. He's to wed Patsy, isn't he?

I was determined to ride this day. In the house, Pa was secured in the front parlor, going over papers for a meeting Mr. Randolph wanted on March 20.

Patsy was likely with him. She was always with him.

"Can I help with the gingerbread?" Betsy came into the kitchen. Her little round face was anxious, asking for my approval, anybody's approval.

"You can make it," I said. "Nancy will be here in a minute and she'll help you."

Pegg's Nancy was almost ready to take over for her mother in the kitchen. She was nine, same as me. We'd long since ceased running about barefoot together, poking into bees' nests. Nancy has been aware of the different roles we have to play out, if I'm not. I'd just as lief be friends with her, but she's done the distancing, not I.

"Did you see Mama this morning?" Betsy asked.

"Yes."

"How is she keeping?"

What if I told her? Mama's in a strait dress, the arms of which are wrapped around and tied behind her, so she can't try to set fire to the house again like she did last week.

But I could not. "She's middling well," I said.

"How long can somebody live with brain fever?"

That was the latest story Pegg had told Betsy and Will. Brain fever. And they had to stay away from her, else they'd catch it.

Two years of brain fever.

"I don't know," I said.

"Why don't you catch it when you go to see her?"

I was ready with the lie. "Because Pegg gives me a special potion so I don't catch it."

She hadn't yet come to the next question, but I expected she would soon: Why can't Pegg give me some of that potion?

I was ready with that lie, too: Because you are too small. It will make you twitch and groan.

God help me for my lies. I'll burn in hell for them one day.

"I must go now," I said. "Here comes Nancy." She was coming down the covered walkway. She was near as tall as her mama already, and her walk just as graceful. "I'll stop by for a piece of that gingerbread when I come back."

"Where you off to?"

You couldn't walk out of a room on Betsy without she didn't ask, "Where you off to?" She was afraid you'd never come back. Pa says it's on account of Mama.

"Riding," I said.

"Patsy won't like it."

"I'm sure she won't. Which is why I shall enjoy it twice as much."

No, Patsy wouldn't like it, I thought as I walked to the stables. She'd say I was filled with "virile boldness" and "daring manliness" and "a breach of modesty." Those are Patsy's words, not mine.

She'd wail that I had no "modest pliancy," that at nine I was already a "hoyden," a "plague," and did not "own a humble distrust of myself."

I am not without "knowledge of my infidelities." But I am very much in possession of my senses. Except for one matter that I cannot get a purchase on, no matter how I try.

When do you keep a secret and when do you tell?

Do you tell the truth, knowing it will hurt someone? Or tell a lie to keep from hurting them? How much does keeping it inside cost? Eventually it will come out, won't it? And hurt the person you are trying to protect, anyway.

Is my lying the worst thing that goes on in this house? No. Madness lives inside our house. Not just in the cellar, where Mama languishes. But the whole house.

Why can't Pa and Patsy see it? I know John sees it, which is why he stays in the stables most of the time. Sometimes he even sleeps in the stables. Tells Pa that Small Hope or one of the others needs him. Pa abides it because he knows John is like Pa's half brother John Syme, Jr., who built a racetrack at Studley Farm, where Pa grew up, and imported blooded stallions to improve the horses in the colony. Sometimes John goes to visit Uncle John. To learn more about horses, he says. I think it's to get away from here.

Sometimes he tells Pa he's going there and goes to visit Dorothea instead.

There's a thunderation. Pa still doesn't know John is seeing Dorothea. Says John is too young for serious courting. At seventeen. Well, I won't scruple or hesitate a moment to lie for John if I have to.

John and I have spoken of the mood that's become a fixture in the house. He thinks he is free of it. And I am not the one to disabuse him of the notion. For believing something is half the battle. And I will deal with God's punishments when they come.

———

THIS DAY JOHN was in the paddock, brushing down Small Hope.

"Hello!" His voice was hearty. He was as tall as Pa now, and broad in the shoulders, too. He wore his hair tied in back in the manner of the day.

"How is she doing?" I asked. I knew he ran her every day.

"She's about in as high perfection as she'll ever be."

Small Hope had won the purse in last fall's four-mile heat in Devil's Field. After that people were starting to respect horses that were Virginia born and bred. And John, as an upcoming horseman.

"I'm riding over to Dorothea's this afternoon," he told me. "Will you explain?"

I said yes. It meant, of course, lying to Pa and Patsy, saying he was riding over to Uncle John's. I saw he had his saddlebags packed with extra clothing.

"You missed breakfast," I said.

He grinned. "Pegg took care of me in the kitchen."

"Pa doesn't like your not being at table with us."

"I know. Here, let me help you mount." And he did.

I looked down from Patches's back at my brother John. He was no longer a boy. I knew how much he loved Dorothea, and I knew she had a lot of beaus.

Suppose she chose somebody else?

I ached for him. We were friends, he and I, cut from the same cloth, of the same mind about so many things. When I was Betsy's age, he'd protected me, even lied for me, often enough to save me from Patsy's wrath. Without him around here, I might indeed go mad.

"Have a good ride," he said. And I said I would. He waved to me and held the gate as I rode Patches out of the paddock.

Sometimes he let me ride Small Hope, while he clocked her. It was our secret. Barley knew but would never tell. And oh, I felt so proud, riding her. So free, and proud because he trusted me with her.

Tucked under me, my skirts exposed my legs up to the thighs. But the warm sun felt good and John paid no mind, except to laugh.

"Your reputation is getting sullied," he said.

Lord knew, he'd heard Patsy's words often enough.

"Yes," I said.

"But you are affable, cheerful, and cleanly industrious, and perfectly qualified to ride Small Hope in the steeplechase. If they let girls do it, I'd let you ride for me."

Oh, and he would, too!

I hadn't worn my riding habit because to go into the house and get it would have meant a confrontation with Patsy.

I cantered across the field, feeling the wind on my face and wishing I was John and could just pack a saddlebag and leave for a day or two.

But I wasn't, and I had to face my own thoughts.

I know Patsy blames Pa for what happened to Mama. But when he comes home, she seeks to reclaim him with smiles and flattery. And Pa allows it because he needs her.

She lies, Patsy does. I've known for a long time that she drinks Mama's tea in secret. And wears her silk when Pa isn't home, and she sits at the head of the table. Oh, she says she doesn't like it, but I know she does. We don't tell, none of us. Which makes us part of her lie. It's important for her to wear that silk dress, I suppose. It makes her feel like the mistress of the plantation.

Well, one red silk dress wasn't going to insure or take away the freedom of the colony. Or even the country.

But her lies have no purpose. And mine do. At least that's what I told myself as I rode across the countryside.

Chapter Fourteen

—

"A NNE, ARE YOU ready? Mr. Thacker is waiting."
"Let him wait."

It was two days later, and Patsy had stepped into my room as I was leaning over to buckle my shoes, after yet another ride.

"Did you wash?" she asked. "Or is Mr. Thacker to be treated to the perfume of horse?"

I straightened up. "If he is, it's a magnificent perfume. Yes, I'm ready. Where are we to do this dolorous act?"

"It isn't dolorous," Patsy explained as she guided me to the front parlor. "Mr. Thacker has ridden here on a snowy, miserable day to buy some of Pa's property along the Holston River."

"Then why doesn't Pa sign Mama's name? He's done it before."

"Ssh!" She shushed me. "That's not to be bandied about. Mr. Thacker does not know Mama is sickly. And he expects two signatures. Now go down and fetch Mama, and bring her to the parlor."

I did so. The fetching part wasn't difficult. Pegg was downstairs already, plying Mama with tea with laudanum in it. Dressing her. Fixing her hair. Mama would have a glazed and distracted look about her, but to the unpracticed eye of a man who would be ushered into a room to meet with her for only five minutes, nothing would be discerned that wasn't ordinary.

"Come on, Mama," I urged, holding her arm and guiding her up the stairs. "Wouldn't you like to take your tea in the parlor?"

"I was in the parlor," she said. Many times she did not know where she was, belowstairs.

"If your pa was here, I wouldn't have to do this," she complained. "He had to go and die and leave legal matters to me. It's never good, a woman having to sign legal papers. Our minds are not fit for such. What property is this man buying?"

"Along the Holston River," I told her.

She humphed. "Got that land from my father, he did. Sheer wilderness out there. Not even under cultivation. Well, I suppose we could use the money. Where is this man? Does he wish to keep me waiting?"

I sat her down in a chair by the window and put a blanket over her knees. "I'll fetch him, Mama."

Pegg stayed with her and I went down the hall to fetch Pa and Mr. Thacker and, of course, Patsy.

———

I WAS GOOD ENOUGH for this, I pondered, as Patsy set down the quill pen and ink and paper on a small table.

"Mrs. Henry, how good of you to give me your time." Mr. Thacker was short and squat and balding. He wore no wig. His suit of clothing was of the plainest linsey-woolsey, which he likely wore to put him in a good light with Pa. He knew better than to show up in any clothing of English cloth or making.

Mama smiled. "Mr. Thacker, that's some wilderness land you wish to buy."

"Well, yes, ma'am. For my sons. I buy it for my sons."

"It was my father's land. My father was a prosperous planter, you know."

"Ah yes, indeed." It was obvious that all Mr. Thacker wanted to know was that Mama would soon sign the deed. Behind him stood Pa, but as usual, Mama never acknowledged Pa's presence. He was dead.

I prayed she wouldn't make mention of that now.

"But he had a penchant for running into debt. My husband bought this property from him, lest the sheriff take possession of it."

"I understand," said Mr. Thacker.

"And now you shall own it. I wish you well with it, Mr. Thacker."

I guided Mama's hand, for it shook. Painstakingly, she wrote out her name. Sarah Shelton Henry.

"If my husband were here he would cry out like a crow that could not fly in a field of corn," she said.

"My wife's recent illness has left her somewhat weakened," I heard Pa whispering to Mr. Thacker.

The paper was signed. Mama sat back in her chair like Queen Charlotte, as if she had just delivered a proclamation. "I shall have another cup of tea now," she directed.

The look in her eyes was one of triumph. And I knew why. Because Pa was "dead" and she had stepped in and taken his place in matters legal.

Mr. Thacker and Patsy left the room. Outside, the snow continued to fall thickly. I shivered, but not from the cold. I shivered because, in my bones, I knew that somehow, in the act of guiding Mama's pen, of propping her up and making her appear normal, I had betrayed her. And become, if only for a few minutes, part of the madness in our house.

———

PA'S FATHER DIED in January. In March, Pa made another one of his successful speeches, and Spencer Roane, who was a friend of John's, came to tell us about it. His father was a burgess from Essex County.

"What a speech your pa made at the last session!" Roane told us. "My father is in a rapture because of it."

We were in our barn. Young Roane loved horses as much as John did. I thought him handsome, and I think he took kind notice of me, too. But I was only ten and still considered a child.

"People are saying that your pa is a man set apart," Roane said. "Edmund Randolph says his imagination paints the soul."

I was at the age when just being near a handsome man made me mindful of all my shortcomings, when I dreamed, for hours after, of how he'd looked and what he'd said.

Roane came to supper. My sister Patsy made him repeat everything being said about Pa. Then she took advantage of the enthusiasm of the moment and asked Pa if she and MyJohn could wed. Pa said yes.

Patsy was nothing if not conniving. She had a fancy wedding that September.

"Do you think it's in keeping with the tone of the times?" MyJohn asked her. "With all the colonies indignant over three pence per pound on the tea?"

Patsy thought so, yes. "It might be the last time we are all together in celebration," she said.

Well, it was in keeping with the tone set by our new governor, Lord Dunmore, anyway. He rode around in a coach given to him by George the Third, just like Mama said he would. They say he is a very good-natured, jolly fellow, who likes his bottle and is known for his midnight sorties.

When my brother John was in Williamsburg for the steeplechase in the summer, he himself saw the governor and his drunken companions clipping the tails of the chief justice's carriage horses. I think the man is more mad than Mama. But, of course, he is a man and in a position of power. Thus he is called a jolly good fellow.

So Patsy had her wedding in the front parlor. Guests feasted out under the trees.

She wore Mama's wedding dress. Blue striped satin,

and pale blue calamanco shoes. I didn't even know Mama had kept these things. And I felt a little jealous because Patsy, as first daughter, got to wear them.

The weather was perfect. Pa's uncle, Reverend Henry, married them. The food was chicken, roast beef, pork, duck, pheasant, oysters, mince pies, custards and blanc-mange, and wedding cake.

Pa was dressed in a manner worthy of his position—a peach-blossom-colored coat and a dark wig tied behind. His mama and two sisters came over from Mount Brilliant for the wedding.

My grandmama is from an old Virginia family. And people sometimes still called her "the Widow Syme," from the name of her first husband. At seventy-five she was feisty as ever. She and her daughters had become Methodist evangelists. Pa's sister Aunt Elizabeth was all the time quarreling with him about my mama, and how he gave her too many children. About neglecting Mama. About slavery. She freed all her slaves.

It made for a lively gathering. Especially with all the talk about the East India Company storing seventeen million pounds of tea in warehouses in England. And having no market for it but America. And wanting us to pay three pence tax per pound for it.

In the coolness of the September afternoon, I'd have paid a three-pence-per-pound tax for a cup of it, without question. I missed my tea.

But then, I had no backbone. Even I knew that.

I think it was the last good time we had in our family. Mama behaved well. Pegg and I dressed her in a good dimity and a lace-trimmed cap. I don't know if she understood what was going on. But she did tell one guest this: "When I married my husband, my dowry was Pine Slash, three hundred acres cut off from the rest of the world."

When Pegg and I put her to bed that night, she smiled at us. "The tea," she said.

"You want tea, Mama?" I asked.

"The water will run brown with it," she said. "And after that, it will run red, with blood of Patriots."

I shivered. "Yes, Mama," I said.

"Don't you ever wed, Anne." She gripped my hand. "Marriage is not a good state. A woman gives up all her property and rights and privileges."

I thought of Spencer Roane. He and his father had been invited to the wedding. He'd sat next to me and talked to me about horses. "It's refreshing to meet a girl who can talk about more than bread pudding," he'd said. And I'd shivered then, and I shivered now.

But again I said, "Yes, Mama." I blew out the candle and left her there in the dark, with her visions of water turning brown from tea, and then red from blood.

———

PATSY CAME BACK from her wedding trip different, worse than before.

She was mistress of Scotchtown now. And everyone must be made mindful of it, from the smallest Negro child on the place to me and Will and, of course, Betsy.

The only one who escaped her mouth was little Edward, who was loved and pampered by everybody.

The first morning back, Patsy made us all stay at the breakfast table after MyJohn kissed her and went to ride his horse out to the fields.

"I am responsible for everyone on this place now. Every time you go farther than the stables or the quarters, I am to know of it. William and Anne, that goes mostly for you two. John, I must be informed of your whereabouts, also."

John sighed, set down his linen napkin, and stood up. "Please, Patsy," he said. "You take yourself too seriously."

She glared up at him. "And what mean you by that?"

"Give the children their rein. They'll be grown up soon enough. Isn't life hard enough for them?" His eyes went to the floor beneath us.

"That is precisely why I must *not* give them rein, John," Patsy said. "And I would appreciate at least being informed when you go to stay the night at the Dandridges."

He shrugged. "You never needed to know before."

"Pa still is not mindful of your courting Dorothea."

"I'm not courting. We're just friends. And Pa knows that."

"Still, he should know how often you go there."

"To what end?" John challenged.

Patsy had no answer.

"You'll not hold sway over me," John said. "And you'd be well advised to loose your grip on Anne."

With that, he turned and strode from the room.

Oh, I thought, as my eyes and my heart followed the tall figure with the broad shoulders and firm feet in those polished boots. Oh, if only I were a boy!

Short of that, if I wished to salvage my own dignity, I must discover, and honor, my true self.

———

RIGHT AFTER PATSY and MyJohn came home, Clementina Rind's husband died. They said it was apoplexy. And, just as Mama had predicted, he left Clementina in debt.

We went to the funeral in town, at Bruton Parish Church. John Pinkney held Clementina's arm. Her children followed the casket up the aisle.

Pegg accompanied me and Patsy. We had to represent the family because Pa was still away and MyJohn too busy.

Afterwards, in the churchyard, I wanted to stand with the Negroes. I liked the way they behaved at funerals better than white people behaved.

Negroes know how to grieve. They fling themselves on the grave of their own. White people just stand there all stiff-faced. And Negroes let their sorrow out in song.

And when they sang, they knew what I was feeling.

But Patsy whispered savagely to me. "Stay where you are. Don't you have any sense of place?"

When everyone went back to the *Gazette* after for a repast, Pegg pitched right in and helped Dick lay out the refreshments.

"Who is putting out the paper today?" Patsy asked.

"Isaac Collins."

Someone took my hand. "You want to see Mr. Collins set the type?" It was Maria, who was about the age of Betsy.

Clementina nodded her permission, and we went into the room where the press was to watch a young man in a white shirt with the sleeves rolled up, a red vest, and his hair tied back. He was sorting type, taking letters from little boxes. Then he would set each letter on an iron rule.

"He's going to put Mama's name on the masthead," Maria told me. "For the first time. My mama is the first woman in the colony to publish a newspaper."

I looked down at her beaming face and thought how open, how free, she seems in comparison to Betsy. And I felt a surge of guilt for my little sister.

And then I thought, how proud this child was of her mother. And I thought of my own.

Mr. Collins smiled at me. "Backwards," he told me. "The type must be set backwards."

When he had a few lines done, he set them in wooden cases that were tied with a string, then locked into an iron frame, and showed it to us before he secured it to the bed of the press.

There it was: PRINTED BY CLEMENTINA RIND.

Then Dick stepped forward to help, using two long-handled, leather-covered ink balls to spread the lampblack over the type.

"Isn't it like magic?" Maria asked me. "Mama says I'm going to help, too, someday."

Behind us I heard Patsy and Clementina. "Who is writing those letters that are signed 'Junius'?" Patsy was asking Clementina.

"I'm not allowed to say. It's part of the secret behind his pen name."

Mr. Collins put moistened sheets of paper in a large frame. "We use about two hundred pounds of pressure to get an impression."

Something was coming alive inside me. Some thought was forming. I nodded politely and smiled.

I'm not allowed to say. It's part of his pen name.

"Would you never tell?" Patsy was asking lightly.

Clementina Rind was solemn. "No. My loyalty is the duty of this paper. Else how could people express themselves about important matters?"

The platen was lowered by Mr. Collins. He held it down about fifteen seconds, then he held up the sheet with the masthead printed on it. Everyone clapped. Maria hugged her mother, who had tears in her eyes. Dick hung up the sheet to dry.

As we left for home Patsy invited, "Come see us whenever you feel the need."

I waved as we drove off, and watched Clementina standing in front of the newspaper office with her children surrounding her. I thought of her words. *Loyalty.* And *duty.* You seldom heard such words from a woman.

Oh, how I wished I had my mama!

My loyalty is the duty of this paper. How else could people express themselves about important matters?

The words stayed in my head.

Chapter Fifteen

———

I MUST CHOOSE a name. I was fired with the idea of it.
I would write a letter to the *Gazette*! Under a pen
name, of course.

I had found a way to take me beyond the pale of
Patsy's dominance, to salvage my own dignity. Even a
way to discover and honor my true self.

Here was something she could not know about. She
may be the mistress of the place, but with a few strokes of
my pen, I could move outside her sway.

What would I write about? I hadn't decided. But the
possibilities were endless. I would read the newspaper
and become acquainted with the issues of the day. Mr.
Chitwell was always admonishing us to read the newspaper.

My words would be in print for all to read and con-
sider and pay mind to. My opinion would matter. Imagine
the freedom of it! The daring!

Mayhap, I thought, as I took a new bay myrtle candle with me to my room that night, mayhap "Junius" is a woman!

———

"ANNE, WHAT ARE you doing up so late?"

Patsy stood in the doorway of my room. She never knocked. In her mind I was not in need of privacy.

"I'm doing some lessons."

She did not believe me. "Why so studious of a sudden?"

"I'm behind in my work," I said. "I don't want Will to get ahead of me."

"He is ahead of you. He has to be to get into Hampden-Sydney next fall."

How I wished *I* could go! Away from here, to live in a school! Hampden-Sydney was eighty miles away. But though Will was only eleven, a professor friend of Pa's was going to prepare him for college. Will was right smart.

"I'll miss him," I said.

"Yes. So will we all. Well, it's near nine. I want that candle out by ten, Anne."

I had an hour. I had decided upon a pen name. "Intrepid." It had a good solid ring to it. And it sounded like a man.

Now all I needed was a subject. The *Gazette* was full of news of the day. Should I write about love and courtship? Many did. About the colonists throwing the tea into the harbor in Boston a week ago?

As I was pondering the matter, a shadow fell across the floor. I looked up. It was Pegg.

"You workin' late. Who you writin' to?"

"I'm doing lessons."

She came in and sat down in a chair and sighed.

"What's wrong, Pegg?" I asked.

"My niece. My sister's girl. Neely. Awhile back she was sold to that Andrew Estave. You know that man your pa talks about? He be in charge of wine? An' the burgesses give him slaves and land and everythin'?"

I remembered. "Virginia's vintner," I said.

"Yeah. That him. She only fifteen. My husband tell me this Estave is a bad man. My niece, Neely, she like my sister. It doan take much to bring her to anger. She already run from this Estave once, and he whip her. Forty lashes."

My eyes went wide. "How do you know all this?"

"When I went with you all to the funeral t'other day. I hear the Negroes talk in town. I'se worried."

"Well, you should be."

"But what kin I do? If your pa was here, I know I could go to him. But he ain't."

Did I dare? Why not? It was better than writing another one about the tea in Boston Harbor. We had evil here right in our own town.

"Mayhap I can help you," I said. "But you mustn't breathe a word of what I am to tell you."

———

I WROTE THE letter that night. And I thought I did rather well.

*It has come to this subscriber's attention
that the colony's vintner, one Andrew Estave,
having been granted land and a number of
slaves to work the vineyards thereon, is none
too appreciative of the value of what has been
bestowed upon him. Would he tear up the vines
of the grapes in the vineyard, because they grow
not fast enough to please him? Or yearn to take
a day just to bask in the sun? No! They are too
tender and dear. Yet when a Negro servant of his,
who is only fifteen years of age, ran from his
brutal treatment, he had administered to her
forty lashes.*

*Are grapevines more dear than a human
being? Mr. Estave's villainy is truly alarming and
this subscriber sorely laments his cruelty. Let his
relations and friends be told he is not acting as a
true son of Virginia. Signed: Intrepid.*

———

I SLIPPED THE letter into the leather fire bucket that sat
outside the front door, where we left the mail.

My letter was printed in the very next issue.

Since I never paid mind to the newspaper, I could not
snatch it up from where it sat with the mail on a table in
the corner of the dining room. I must wait for MyJohn to
go through the mail when we had our noon meal.

MyJohn, who never sat in Pa's place at the table,
would go through the mail quickly, hand all invitations,
family letters, and the paper to Patsy, sit down, spread

open his napkin, and say, "Well, young Henrys, and tell me what you all have been up to this morning?"

MyJohn was working harder than ever in helping Mr. Melton run the place now. And we children all still adored him. He was the one we went to when Patsy was unduly harsh. On occasion, I knew, he spoke to her of her harshness, especially with Betsy. But never in front of us.

"May I see the *Gazette*?" I asked him.

"Only Pa is allowed to read the paper at the table," Patsy said.

"As soon as we are finished, you may have it, yes," MyJohn said.

"You have chores this afternoon, don't you, Anne?" Patsy asked. "No paper until your chores are finished."

But when we left the room, MyJohn winked at me and handed me the paper behind Patsy's back. "Just put it back with Pa's mail," he said.

It was there, my letter. I sat on my bed and let the lines of *my words* bore into my brain. There they were. My own words! No one had questioned them, or my right to put them there. I had been treated, by the paper, like every other citizen.

I was so proud I thought I would burst. And somehow, when I could, I would show the words to Pegg. She couldn't read, of course, but she could understand. And she could be grateful.

———

THE LETTER CHANGED nothing in my life. I did not really expect it to. Patsy still ruled the house with an iron hand. Betsy became ever more docile and solemn. John still stayed out in the barn most of the time working with his horses. Will buried his nose in his books and grew away from me because he must be ready for college.

No one responded to the letter in the *Gazette*.

My spirit was cast down. "Why doesn't anyone write an answer to it, at least?" I asked Pegg one day in the kitchen.

She was chopping vegetables. "People saw it," she said. "You gots to be patient."

"Likely nobody even read it."

She stopped chopping. "I know that ain't true."

She knew things; I was sensible of that. If you thought the Negro servants weren't aware of what was going on, just because they didn't speak of events, you were a fool by half.

"Tell me," I said.

She slid her eyes around to make sure no one was in hearing distance. "You keep a still tongue in your head?"

"Why wouldn't I? Who would I tell to?"

"My husband, he say Mr. Estave be furious 'bout that letter."

"How would your husband know?"

But she just shook her head. "We know things, Anne. We keep in touch with Negroes in town and on other plantations. We gots to do this. Doan you worry; your letter did good." Then she picked up a tomato. "You see this. When was it planted?"

"Months ago."

"With what?"

I shrugged. "Seeds."

"Well then?" She smiled. "You just look at that letter of yours like a seed. It could take months to grow."

She was right, only it didn't take that long. Two months later, Pegg told me her niece had run off again. And how worried she was about her.

I scanned the next issue of the *Gazette* and read the notice about her to Pegg.

> *Run away from the subscriber, a mulatto wench, name of Neely. She is but fifteen years of age, about five feet high, and well made. Wearing, when she left, a good pair of pink-colored worsted stockings and good leather shoes, a Virginia cloth jacket, Kersey wove, and a striped petticoat. I will give a reward of twenty pounds to who delivers her to me. Andrew Estave.*

"That be her," Pegg told me. "I pray nobody hands her over."

But they did. A week later Pegg told me she had heard at church that Neely was once again returned to Mr. Estave and once again suffered forty lashes.

I wrote another letter. Pa was not yet back. I made it strong. I asked, "What cruelty makes this young girl run?" And, "at what cost the wine from grapes grown in Virginia?"

I made bold to suggest that the House of Burgesses, that had provided Mr. Estave with his plantation and slaves to grow Virginia grapes, might do well to cast an eye on how he conducted himself.

I never thought Patsy would find out. Like as not, I'd have done it anyway, just to plague her. But I never thought she would find out, is all.

Chapter Sixteen

December 1773

I T WAS MRS. HOOPER who told her. Old Mrs. Hooper, with a face like a ferret, who came around with her copy of the *Gazette* in hand just before Christmas, bearing the news that Neely was none other than the niece of our Pegg.

"How nice of you to call!" Patsy stood on the front steps as the carriage with the crest on the side pulled up in the roundabout. "Come in. I'll have Jane make some chocolate."

The ferret's footman helped her down. She was given to fat. Her stomacher was near bursting in front. "Isn't this a lovely day? Is your father home from Williamsburg yet?"

"No," from Patsy. "Do come in, the house is nice and warm."

She stepped inside and looked around with her beady eyes. I could swear she was sniffing.

"My, you do look handsome," Patsy said, admiring her gown.

Old Ferret Face pulled herself up straight, and silk swished. "This is an old gown."

It didn't look old to me.

"We do not anymore import English goods, as the *Gazette* reports. That was a villainous list that woman printed. Shows what happens when women are given power. It near ruined our reputation hereabouts."

Patsy pretended surprise.

"I am a good citizen. As is my whole family. But I wish I could say the same for yours!"

She sat down heavily in the chair I pulled out for her at the dining room table. Jane was already scurrying around, setting out cups for hot chocolate and cake.

"Have you a complaint about us?" Patsy asked with politeness.

Mrs. Hooper waited until Jane had left the room. "We must be careful these days. There are rumors of a slave insurrection in nearby Surrey County. And reports of them meeting secretly in Williamsburg."

She turned the pages of the *Gazette* and my heart flipped. There she found my latest letter.

Patsy read it. "What has this to do with us?"

"You truly don't know? This slave girl the subscriber writes about here is a niece of your Pegg," Mrs. Hooper said.

Patsy gasped. "How come you to this conclusion?"

"This girl Neely was about our place when she last ran off. Thought it was Scotchtown. She told my Scipio that she was looking for her aunt Pegg at Scotchtown. Now, Patsy Henry, tell me someone here did not write this letter? I know your father has subversive ideas, but even he must cooperate with his neighbors if we are to keep these people in line."

"Our slaves cannot read or write, Mrs. Hooper," Patsy said. "And neither I nor MyJohn wrote it."

———

WHEN SHE TOOK her leave, Mrs. Hooper looked at Patsy. "There are rumors about in the neighborhood that there is a crazy woman in the cellar here in Scotchtown."

I saw Patsy's face go white. "What kind of person speaks such horrible things of us?"

"I know it is your mama."

"My mama isn't crazy," I blurted out.

Patsy shushed me.

"People are saying," Mrs. Hooper went on, "that your pa hands her food down to her through a trapdoor when he is home."

I thought Patsy would faint.

"And if you do not punish whoever wrote this, and see it does not happen again, I will tell what I know to be true."

She went out the door. "He may be a good speaker, your pa, and a good politician, but if he allows the Nigras hereabouts to be incited, nothing he says will be paid mind to."

Right after supper, MyJohn asked me to accompany him and Patsy into the front parlor. I'd just decorated it with greens and winter berries for Christmas. The smell of fresh greens was everywhere.

He closed the door. In his hand he had the *Gazette*. "Did you write this, Anne?" he asked gently.

I could not lie to MyJohn. I would not. So I said yes.

Patsy stamped her foot and started to pace. "I knew it!" she snapped. "And the last one, too?"

"Yes," I said.

"Why?" she demanded.

"Do you want the truth?" I glared at my sister.

"We always want that, Anne," MyJohn said.

Did they? When they got it, they could not abide it. "I did it to do something outside your hold on me," I told Patsy. "And I did it to help Neely. And Pegg."

"Do you see what I have to contend with? She did it to plague me!" Patsy said.

"Pa's always fighting battles for people," I said. "What's so bad about what I did?"

MyJohn gave Patsy a look then, and she stamped out of the room. Then he put his hand on my shoulder and led me to the settee. "Anne, I know things are difficult in this house. I know, without undermining her authority, that Patsy sometimes takes on about small things. But she is terrified."

"About what?"

"That you will turn out like your mother."

"She's going to make me, if she doesn't stop with her meanness."

"She's only trying to help you."

I glared at him. "You believe that?"

He did not answer. And it was then that it came to me, an early, bitter knowledge. Men are helpless in the face of the women they love. They can do nothing!

"Anne, you mustn't write any more letters. Promise me. This letter you wrote will only serve to embarrass your father. As a member of the House of Burgesses, he was instrumental in giving Mr. Estave the land and slaves."

"Do you think Mr. Estave should be allowed to treat Neely like that?"

"No. And as soon as your father comes home I'll speak to him of the matter. I promise. But you must promise, too. No more letters."

"Do you think that's why Pa and the others are in meetings now?" I put to him. "So we can be suppressed from our freedoms?"

"You are too smart by half," he said. "And it's why Patsy fears for you. You'll find grief in the world, my girl, if you don't curb that willful nature." He was not joking.

Then he had a thought. "I want to be fair with you. What say you enter the poetry contest Mrs. Rind runs every year?"

I shrugged. "Patsy enters it."

"She'd be proud if you won. Will you try?"

A poetry contest! But MyJohn had promised to speak to Pa about the way Mr. Estave treated Neely. And I knew he would keep his promise. So I'd accomplished something after all.

"All right," I said. "But remember to speak to Pa."

RIGHT AFTER CHRISTMAS I wrote a poem and entered it in the contest.

> *When a woman's face is wrinkled*
> *And her hairs are sprinkled,*
> *With gray, Lackaday!*
> *Like fashions past,*
> *Aside she's cast,*
> *No one respect will pay;*
> *Remember, Lasses, remember.*
> *And while the sun shines make hay:*
> *You must not expect in December,*
> *The flowers you gathered in May.*

I won the contest. I won a new parasol and was allowed to select any book I wanted from the *Gazette* office.

Patsy wanted me to pick *Pilgrim's Progress.* I picked *Paradise Lost,* by John Milton. Patsy wouldn't show me the poem she entered, and I knew she would never forgive me for winning.

Chapter Seventeen

———

SEPTEMBER 1774

THIS YEAR, the year of '74, was the worst ever in my life.

The water in Maryland, where Patriots had set fire to a tea ship, burned brown as the tea went into the harbor.

The British closed the Port of Boston and the mood of the people was soured.

Pa was one of the delegates from Virginia to Philadelphia for the Continental Congress. It was two days' ride to Colonel Washington's home at Mount Vernon, where he was going first. He'd travel to Philadelphia with Colonel Washington and a man by the name of Pendleton.

After he left, Patsy acted as if the trouble that brought about such a Congress was the fault of us younger ones. She took it upon herself to make sure we knew what was going on in the colonies. She'd walk into the parlor in the midst of our lessons, interrupt Mr. Chitwell, and ask us things like:

"You know why Pa has gone to Philadelphia? Why the Congress must meet? Now, see what's happened. You children will grow up now."

There was war right here in our house.

Lines had been drawn on the heart-pine floor. John stayed more and more in the stables. He had a small room there for himself now.

MyJohn found himself in the middle of the turmoil, but I suspected he leaned more to us younger ones. Several times he took up for us.

Betsy's face grew thinner every day. Will bent to his books. I knew he was hoping to be allowed to go to his private tutor at Hampden-Sydney even sooner if he passed certain exams.

When you have people at war with each other in your own house, you haven't time for the mischief those in power are making on the outside.

———

AND THEN, Clementina Rind died of consumption. She'd worked so hard the last year to pay back the debts left to her by her husband that her body pure gave out. We went to her funeral. I think all of Williamsburg was there. I knew we had all lost a friend.

———

"PA, THERE's a British ship that's moored at Yorktown," John said.

We were at supper. Pa had been home since the first of November. It was the next-to-last day of that month.

"I know of it, John," Pa answered.

"Spencer Roane said there's a horse aboard. Name of Doormouse. His sire was Woodpecker; his dam, Juno. He's chestnut, stands fourteen hands. Few Arabians are taller. He ran undefeated in four races, including the Great Subscription Purse in York, England. Pa?"

"Why is he here?" Pa asked.

"He was imported by John Hoomes, of this colony. Hoomes can't afford him now."

Pa nodded. "Hoomes is a tobacco farmer, son. They're not exporting to England, so he's not getting his two pence per pound."

"Pa, I've saved my money from the purse Small Hope won. I could buy this horse. I'm sure the price will be lowered."

Everyone at the table looked first at John, then at Pa. Buy? From England?

I held my breath. John's eyes were bright with anticipation. Pa took a sip of wine. "Are you to be one of our rascals, then?" he asked.

John blushed. At the Congress in Philadelphia, Pa had suggested that the date for importing English goods should be put off until December 1, instead of November 1.

"We don't mean to hurt even our own rascals, if we have any," he'd said.

The Congress had agreed. December 1 was the last date to buy anything imported from England. And here now was this ship moored at Yorktown, ten miles down-river from Williamsburg, and the closest deepwater harbor. It had a customs house, a tobacco warehouse.

And here was this horse.

And there was my brother John, polite, respectful, yearning, with mayhap his last chance to acquire a horse with such a bloodline, for years.

"I could breed him. With Uncle John's Druid. Uncle John says," he started, but Pa held up a hand to stop him.

"I have no doubt what my half brother says. All right, then, but how do you propose to do this without letting the whole county know about it?"

"The Committee says it's all right. That anybody buying isn't going against the nonimportation agreement."

We had committees now. It was part of taking the government into our own hands. Pa had been busy all month, organizing. He was now also captain of the Hanover Volunteers. They mustered at Smith's Tavern. John and MyJohn were members.

"I know that, John. If it were, I wouldn't allow it. But you're still my son. And we haven't imported anything from England in years. Why, Patsy here hasn't had a silk dress in how long now?"

"Yes, she has," I blurted out.

Patsy gasped. I didn't care. It did my heart good to say it. She'd come down on me hard since the business with the letter writing, and I was determined to get back at her. "She's got a silk dress. Made it in secret. And she wears it when you're not here, Pa."

His scowl darkened. But not at Patsy; at me. "I'll warrant it's from silk she'd long since laid by," he said. "And that she hasn't worn it outside this house. Am I right, Patsy?"

"Yes, Pa," she said quietly.

"And we do not tell tales on each other in this house, Anne." His voice was gentle, but I could not abide him scolding me. Tears came to my eyes.

"Again, how do we justify this, John?" he asked my brother.

John's shoulders slumped. "I've worked so hard for years, Pa. It's my livelihood. I've never asked for anything. It's my last chance to get a horse imported from England."

Pa nodded and sighed. "Yes, all right, then. You may go to Yorktown with Spencer, if you wish, and buy this horse. But don't bandy it about."

"Thank you, sir." John beamed across the table at me. Then he sobered. "May I take Will with me?"

"Will has his college exams tomorrow," Patsy reminded him.

I saw Will's face drop.

"How about Anne?"

Pa scowled.

"It doesn't make a particle of sense to take Anne. She has duties," Patsy scolded.

But Pa held up his hand to let John finish.

"I may need help," John said.

"You have Spencer."

"Well, Anne knows horses and she never gets to go anywhere, Pa. She's been working so hard, carding and weaving. None of us would have the clothes we're wearing if she didn't."

It was true. Patsy had me carding, spinning, weaving, even bleaching the finished cloth. After the business with the letter writing, she'd increased my work until I felt like a drone.

To my surprise, Pa let me go. Over Patsy's objections. Sometimes I think he knew more than he let on, my pa, more than the rest of us thought he did.

———

I KNEW, RIGHT OFF, that John had a plan, that he wasn't asking for me for company. He soon told me.

We packed for the ride. I wore my warmest riding habit. We'd stay the night at Mrs. Barrow's on the way, and at an inn in Williamsburg. "I'm trusting you with your sister," Pa told John. "She's to have her own room in both places."

Outside, the sky was bright November blue, but the trees were near bare and the wind was cold.

Our ride was great sport. Spencer Roane seemed glad for my company and complimented me on my riding.

But we had a secret this day, my brother John and I, and I suppose he had already shared it with Spencer.

I had brought along a pair of John's old britches, shirt, vest, and jacket. It turned out that my brother needed me to act for him.

"Spencer doesn't approve," John told me. "But he's promised not to tell."

I was so excited I could scarce keep my horse in rein. Spencer pretended to be shocked at just seeing me ride astride.

"I most often ride bareback," I teased him.

"She's a wanton," John said.

"And you're not helping to keep her in line," he answered.

We had a pleasant stay at Mrs. Barrow's, a good breakfast, and the weather held the next day. We spent the night at The Sign of the Dolphin in Williamsburg, and that night there was a frolic and I got to dance with Spencer before John made me go to bed. The next day I smelled the water of the James before I saw it. I saw the tall sails of the *Deborah* from a distance away, with sailors hallooing to us from the shrouds, as if we were old friends.

Oh, it was so good to be away from Scotchtown, away from the wool carding, the knitting, my studying, and needlework. I felt so free and alive! And then I thought of Mama, imprisoned in the cellar, and I felt guilty.

Before we got to the wharf, John signaled that we should duck behind a copse of trees so I could shed my riding habit and put it in my saddlebag. Under the habit this day I had on my boy's clothing.

John took a tricorn hat and bade me tuck my hair up and put it on.

"How do I look?"

I saw Spencer Roane's eyes go over me.

"You look the part," John said. "Remember, now, you can't write. The factor will likely ask you to make your mark."

I nodded.

Spencer shook his head. "You two," he said in mock despair. But as he turned to mount his horse, I saw he was smiling.

———

WE DISMOUNTED NEAR some crates just off the wharf and stood watching for a few minutes.

British soldiers were guarding the walkway to the ship. And members of the Committee—Virginians in hunting shirts, carrying muskets—were holding back the crowd of bewigged gentlemen and ladies accompanied by Negro servants holding baskets, waiting for the goods to be unloaded.

Factors, men who acted as go-betweens, stood on the foredeck. Of a sudden, the crowd started chanting, "Salt, salt, salt, salt."

I looked at Spencer. "The colony is short of salt," he said. "There's supposed to be twenty-four hundred bushels aboard. And Madeira. And silks in great plenty, as well as Irish linens and a lot of other furbelows the ladies hereabouts have been dying for."

"And one horse, pray," John said.

I heard the sound of the water gently lapping around the pilings, the buzz of talk, the cry of vendors selling gingerbread. Dogs ran in and about the crowd, along with children. There was a general excitement in the air. No one recognized me.

John pressed the purse of money into my hands and bade me put it into my haversack. I did so.

The captain of the ship was talking with the head of the Committee. "My ship needs repairs," he said. "My men need a day ashore to acquire some provisions for the trip home."

Someone pointed to the road and a wagon coming, loaded with chickens and pigs, potatoes. Another was behind it with barrels of water and beer.

The Committee let the wagons through and only then did the captain allow members of the Committee, and some important-looking gentlemen, to board her.

Then the head of the Committee read an announcement, allowing those who had ready money to file aboard in an orderly manner.

All were men. "Don't forget, at least three yards," I heard one woman calling after her husband.

"We need that Madeira for Christmas entertaining," said another.

John squeezed my hand. "Will you be all right?"

"Yes."

"I'd do it myself, but it's as I thought. I know all the Committee men."

"I'll keep." And I filed aboard with the rest of them. Once up on deck John and Spencer seemed so far below. But I didn't take time to look around. John had told me what to do, who to see. A Mr. Humphries, one of the English factors.

"He'll be near the hold," John had said. And he told me where the hold was on the ship.

And there he was, a tall thin man in an outlandish yellow frock coat. I headed straight for him but was barred by a burly seaman. "You got business here, boy?"

"Yes sir." I tried to make my voice deep. "I'm here to see Mr. Humphries. I've come for Mr. Henry, my master. For a horse, name of Doormouse. Chestnut he is. Supposed to be sold to Mr. Hoomes of this colony, but he hasn't the cost of her. Mr. Henry would buy her in his stead."

He looked at Mr. Humphries, who nodded, and I went toward him. "You've got the king's shilling?"

"Yes sir." I reached into my haversack and pulled out the small leather purse and shook it.

"Mr. Henry!" Humphries rubbed his chin. "That wouldn't be Mr. Patrick Henry, the troublemaker, the man your royal governor calls a man of desperate circumstances, now, would it?"

"No sir. There be many Henrys in Virginia."

He opened the purse, looked at the money, then ordered that the horse be brought up the ramp from the hold.

While we waited, he told me how they had been three months and three days at sea. "'Tis a beautiful place this Virginia," he said. "I've been here but once, but I always wanted to come back for good someday. Now, with war coming, it looks as if that's been denied to me.

But I'm determined to get ashore this day for some good vittles."

Then I heard the footfalls of a horse coming up a ramp, a whinny. And out into the sunlight stepped Doormouse, the most beautiful horse I'd ever seen.

I had all I could do to keep my hands off his shining coat. John had warned me not to appear too anxious.

Mr. Humphries took some papers from his pocket. "How much did your master say to pay?"

I told him.

He grunted. "It's thievery. But if the weather's bad, he could break a leg on the journey home and my client will then have naught for his trouble. Can you make your mark?"

I said yes. His assistant held the ink pot for me, and I dipped the quill pen in and made an X on the important-looking paper.

"Ye've got a fine horse there." Mr. Humphries patted Doormouse, then directed his assistant to lead him down the gangway.

"I can do it, sir," I said.

But he shook his head. "I deliver onto Virginia soil in one piece," he said. "And I'll be right behind you. I'm determined to have myself a good meal while I'm here if I have to shoot the wild turkey myself."

———

I SHALL NEVER forget the look on John's face as Mr. Humphries' assistant handed over the bridle to him, and I handed over the papers.

He was so busy patting Doormouse and examining his flanks, remarking on his beautiful conformation and proud carriage, he scarce thanked me. Spencer did. He put his arms around me in what he thought was a generous brotherly hug.

It was anything but to me. And it completed the sweetness of the day. And Spencer never told my secret, which made us friends of a truer nature.

Chapter Eighteen

February 1775

DOORMOUSE WAS THE only happy thing to come to us that year of '74. John often allowed me and the younger children to ride him. The younger ones he oversaw, of course. I was allowed just to ride him around the paddock at first, but once he saw I could keep my seat, he allowed me out on the familiar paths he rode. As long as I did not race.

John raced. And watching him was like seeing a flight of an eagle, straight and true and filled with purpose.

I took joy in watching him. And every time I looked at Doormouse, I remembered that time I spent with John and Spencer. I saw myself in boys' clothing, and I knew I had done something to discover my true self.

It was a good thing I had done, but it was another lie. Another secret to keep.

But we kept secrets well in that house. We walked around, all of us, with our secrets. And our lies.

———

IT CAME SOMEHOW to be February of the next year. Nothing had changed. Mama was still in the cellar, but she was more angry at us all, even, betimes, violent.

She needed laudanum most of the time now. And she looked at you like her eyes were prison gates, and she was held against her will behind them.

Pa was seldom home.

John spent more time than ever in the stables when he wasn't practicing with the militia. Will studied all the time, and Betsy was growing more solemn by the moment.

Sometimes I saw Spencer Roane when he came to visit John and the horses. Always he had time to speak to me, to ask after me, and at Christmastime he came to visit with his father and brought me a book, and sat next to me by the fireside while Pa played the violin. And the looks that passed between us were like a path cleared across a wild forest, though I was not yet twelve.

But he, too, was coming into a man's estate and must satisfy his tutor's demands. He would go to the college in Williamsburg, then read law.

I looked forward to his visits.

Then, one February night, Mama looked queerly at me when I brought down her supper.

"You're dead," she said.

The words struck me like a blow in the face. I set down the dish. "No, Mama, I'm here. Alive."

"Dead." She spat out the word. "Just like your pa."

Pa was the only other member of the family she'd pronounced dead so far. And now me.

I left the food. I fled upstairs. I went into the back parlor where Patsy, Will, and the others were gathered. I said nothing.

———

THE HOUSE SEEMED filled with shadows more than usual that February night. It was not where I wanted to be. Wind beat about the shuttered windows. The fire crackled.

I wanted to be in the barn with the horses, where the smell of hay sweetly mingled with the smell of leather and horse. Where they were all alive and warm. And waiting.

For the future. Waiting to run into the future and carry us with them.

That is why John loves them, I thought. They are the future. And they take him away from here and make him free.

Patsy was playing the pianoforte, Will attempting to study, Betsy reading, and little Edward playing with wooden blocks on the floor.

I looked at all of them as if I'd never seen them before. All seemed beautiful to me, even Patsy.

Will I soon die? I asked myself. Mama had the sight. Oh God, I didn't want to die. Bad as life was betimes, I wanted to live and wed and have children, I did.

I knew it then, knew I would someday marry.

Knew it would be Spencer Roane.

Pa and MyJohn and John were at Colonel Overton's house for supper. Overton was a friend and neighbor. And he was a colonel because sooner or later all Virginia's landed gentry got to be called colonel.

"I should have gone with Pa and the others tonight," Will said, so softly that Patsy couldn't hear it.

We were in the back parlor because Patsy insisted we all be about our affairs in one room at night. She said it was to save candlelight. I think it was so she could keep us all under her nose.

"You have your studies," she told Will.

"I passed my exams for college."

"You still must study."

"Well, I'm a man. Or near one. And I should be allowed to join the militia with MyJohn and John, too."

"No need for you to be part of these mournful events yet, Will," she said. "Anyway, the ages for militia are sixteen to fifty."

"I'm bigger than some of the sixteen-year-olds. And a better shot."

Patsy sighed. "Take up a lantern, why don't you, and go to the door. I think it's Pa and the boys now."

Will did so. And there was much stamping of feet and stout talk as they came in. Patsy sent Pegg for coffee and biscuits and ham.

"We've scarce eaten," MyJohn said, taking off his scarf and warming his hands before the fire. "The talk was so rich at Colonel Overton's nobody had time for food."

Little Edward scrambled to be taken up in Pa's arms.

Betsy stayed put. She used to do that, run to Pa soon as he came in, but now she considered it unladylike.

"What talk?" Patsy commenced to serve coffee. My-John sneaked a biscuit off a silver tray. Pa sat with Edward on his lap, and Patsy motioned for Pegg, who came in with a bowl of hot punch, to take off Pa's boots.

But I knelt to do so before Pegg had a chance to put the punch bowl down. Pa put his hand on my head as I did so and ruffled my hair.

"Your father said that if hostilities soon commence, France, Spain, and Holland, the natural enemies of Great Britain, will come to our aid," MyJohn recited. "That Louis the Sixteenth shall be satisfied by our declaration of independence, but not until then will he send his fleet and arms to help us."

Patsy gasped. "Independence! Pa, you said the word? Truly?"

Pa was sipping his coffee, surrounded by his family. "Truly," he said.

"Why, it's a hobgoblin of so frightful an idea that it would throw a delicate person into fits to look it in the face!" Patsy said.

MyJohn put a hand around her shoulder. "Then, don't look it in the face," he said gently. "Look at me, instead. I've something more to tell you."

"What?"

"All the assembled gentlemen gave a toast. To you."

"To me?" Patsy's hand went over her heart in mock dismay.

"Yes, they all agreed that without you to take care of his home and family, Mr. Henry would not have been able to serve Virginia as he has done. They toasted your health. And God's shoe buckles, I was proud."

Patsy ran to Pa, and he embraced her. Then she embraced each of us, in turn.

Tears came to my eyes. Patsy will be remembered as the one who made it possible for Pa to help the colony to declare itself free, I thought. And what will I be remembered for? The girl who brought supper down to her mama in the cellar? Lordy, we'll never be able to live with Patsy now.

———

When the others went off to bed, Will lingered, wanting to talk to Pa. I wanted to, also, but I waited out in the hall.

I couldn't help listening, could I?

"Pa, can't I join the militia? I'm strong enough and big enough."

Pa said something to soothe him over. The talk was low, but I heard the words "man of the place" and "if we're all gone." Will came out of the room, books in hand, head held high, and walked right by me in the hall. I stepped back into the room.

Pa had a way about him of making each of us feel we were important to him. Even now, when Patsy had been toasted for being the one whose efforts had allowed him to continue with his work.

Was Pa lying? When do you tell the truth and when do you lie? When do you keep a secret? Are all secrets to be kept?

I went into the room. "Pa?"

"Ah, yes, Anne, come here. You looked so cast down before. Don't take on about the toast for Patsy. All of you make it possible for me to do my work."

"It isn't that, Pa."

"What, then?"

"When I brought Mama her supper, she asked for you this day."

He nodded. "Do you think she's still awake?"

"She walks the floor half the night," I told him.

He sighed heavily.

"Pa, this night she said something terrible to me."

"And what is that, Anne?"

"She said I was dead."

"Well," and he smiled, "you're in good company, then. I'm dead, too, you know."

"Oh, Pa!" I burst out crying, and he held me close to him on the settee. "There, there, child, that is why your mama is in the cellar, among other reasons."

"But she has the sight, Pa. Do you think I shall soon die, then?"

"One day we will all be dead, Anne," he said gravely. "She is right about that. No, I do not think you will soon die, however. I think you grow more comely every day, and shall live a long and happy life."

"Pa, why are things so bad around here?"

"Our family is broken, Anne. It happens betimes with families. So what we must do is know that while other families get to enjoy the whole, we can only enjoy the pieces. But don't hold them too close. Broken pieces have edges and can hurt. Look outside the family for your happiness."

Then he released me, stood up, and separated himself from the shadows, and I saw how tired he looked. "How has she been, Anne? I'll go and see her now, child. Thank you. Go to bed."

———

BUT I DID not go to bed. I stayed outside the door that led to the cellar.

And that was when I heard it. I know I did.

I heard Mama say it.

When I told Patsy she said no. And that if I breathed a word of what I thought I heard Mama say, or what I had lied about what I heard Mama say, she'd punish me severely.

Miss Importance was so filled up with herself now, she thought nobody else responsible for the good things Pa had done but her.

But Mama said it. I know she did.

———

HE WAS DOWN there a long time. I heard their voices, muffled by the thick door so I could not hear the words, but I knew the tones. His low and placating. Hers shrill and begging.

And then her voice became even more shrill. She was screaming something, in begging tones.

It was then that I heard her say it.

"Patrick, Patrick, please, I beg of you, give me my freedom, or let me go to my death!"

Over and over she said it, she sobbed it. And Pa came back with quiet words. For he was looking at a hobgoblin of so frightful an idea that it would throw anyone into fits to look it in the face.

I never went downstairs to see my mama after that night.

Chapter Nineteen

———

WHY AIN'T YOU BEEN down to see your mama?" Pegg asked me two days after.

But I did not answer.

"She askin' fer you."

Still, I did not answer.

We were in the traveler's room, where she was setting out vittles for the others when they came home from church. I had slept late. The last two days I had conjured up a low fever, and Pa did not want me outside, where it was snowing and the sky was so gray and low I wished it would cover me over like a blanket.

"She wants to die," I finally said.

Near the hearth Pegg set down a pewter bowl of steaming biscuits covered with a white linen napkin. "Ask me, I'd say, let her die, poor soul. What she got to live for?"

"Not that," I said. "She wants to die to be free. I'm

afraid she'll ask me to give her something to make her die."

"Lord take her when He ready," she told me. Then she left the room. I took a hot biscuit and gazed into the fire, wondering when He was going to be ready.

———

THE FAMILY CAME home in a double gig. Grandma, Aunt Lucy, and Aunt Jane were with them. I jumped up to greet them.

Grandma and the others stayed two days and brought with them the outside world, robust and hearty.

We pulled taffy. We sang sacred music that night around the fire while Pa played his violin. Grandma told stories about Pa as a boy, how he'd made a "slope," a fish trap, across a branch of the Staunton River, and kept his family in fish.

How he loved hunting deer and hollowed out a canoe from a single log.

I didn't think about death when Grandma was around. She knew French, and taught us a game called "Cries of Paris." We children had been taught French by our tutor, though it was not very good.

But with her game, we learned more. Grandma had so many games that had to do with words and learning that I wished she could be our tutor.

What was to be the last evening of their visit, when Pegg went down to bring Mama's supper, Grandma was showing us how to engrave eggshells.

Of a sudden I heard Pegg running up the stairs, through the hall, and out the back door, banging it behind her. I knew something was wrong and went to wait by the back door. Pa was in the barn with MyJohn and John, because one of John's horses was dropping a foal.

How long I waited, I don't know. I heard Grandma's voice from the parlor. "We must let the egg soak in the vinegar until those parts not touched with tallow will stand out from the shell. It is called 'relief.'"

Then I saw the lantern Pa was holding as he came through the snow with Pegg.

"What's happened?" I asked when they came through the door.

Pegg gave me a look. "The window be broken down there. I find a pile of snow on the floor. Your mama huddled in her bed, coughin'."

———

PA SENT FOR Dr. Hinde, who first said it was an ague, then a distemper of the throat and chest.

Pa was so agitated we kept out of his way. "Who untied her strait dress?" He gathered us older ones together. Grandma stood between me and Betsy, her hand on our shoulders.

"Anne and Pegg are the only ones who go down there besides you, Pa," Patsy said.

Oh, she was quick to lay blame.

Pa looked at me.

"I haven't been down in two days."

His eyes narrowed. "Why?"

I shrugged and looked at the floor.

"I'm afraid I've been keeping them too busy," Grandma answered for me.

I'd never told anyone but Pa that Mama had said I was dead. I couldn't. If I did, Patsy wouldn't believe I was the one to inherit the bad blood. You had to grow up to inherit it.

I had to keep her believing that, for my own purposes.

I hadn't told anyone but Pegg what Mama had said about wanting her freedom or wanting to die. And Pa didn't know I'd heard it.

"Pegg?" Pa looked at her.

I saw that Pegg's amber eyes were steady, so, too, the voice. "No, Master, I never loosened the dress. But she tol' me she knew how to do it."

Was this true? Had Pegg loosened the strait dress to help Mama hurt herself?

If so, it was my fault, for telling her Mama wanted to die, wasn't it?

When do you tell the truth and when do you lie? There it was again. Do you tell a lie, like I did about inheriting the bad blood, to keep someone from harm?

Do you tell the truth, like I told Pegg about Mama wanting to die? And see that truth mayhap come to hurt someone?

Dr. Hinde bled Mama. Pegg was to stay the night with her. Dr. Hinde stayed, too, sleeping in the traveler's room.

Pa sat up in the chair in front of the hearth in the parlor and finally fell asleep there. Everyone else went to bed. The house got quiet, except for the sound of rain now, freezing rain, against the windows.

I sat on the floor with my head leaning on a chair in the same room with Pa. I slept that way all night, waked every so often by visions and voices of my family. Charger sat next to me. When I woke, I'd put another log on the fire.

Early the next morning, in the dimness of a gray-frozen time, I was the one who heard Dr. Hinde come into the parlor. He looked disheveled and tired.

He came to Pa's chair and put a hand on his shoulder. "Mr. Henry," he said.

Pa woke, startled. "Does she still live?"

"She's suffering from a violent inflammation of the membranes of the throat," he said. "Her throat is near closed. The end is near."

Pa called the rest of them from their rooms, and they came, wrapped in sleep as well as their dressing robes. We all went belowstairs to sit around Mama's bed. Patsy must be the closest to her, of course.

Mama could not talk. Her eyes went from one of us to the other. How like a trapped animal she looks, I thought. She does not know us. She wonders who we are. Is my own dear mama somewhere in that feverish body?

John came close and held me. Patsy was praying from the Bible. The sound of Mama's rasping breath filled the room. Then it stopped. And very soon the doctor stepped forward and closed her eyes.

"Oh, my mama, my mama!" Patsy screamed. And she threw herself on Mama. MyJohn had to draw her away.

It was Grandma and I who held little Edward, Betsy, Will, and John. And I thought, well, isn't she our mama, too?

Chapter Twenty

—

WE BURIED MAMA in the cemetery at Mount Brilliant on a February day that the wind whipped around us the way March wind was supposed to do.

It was Grandma and Grandpa's place. Grandpa had been laid to rest in the same cemetery.

We huddled in the cold together while Reverend Henry read words that were snatched from his mouth, and Pa stood by looking like he was walking in his sleep and trying to figure out how he ended here at his pa's grave.

I wondered if Mama had found her freedom now, if she was happy. I wondered if Pa was thinking that it was the same freedom he went speechifying about, if her words about wanting to die, without it, went through his head.

Edward and Betsy stood close to me. Every so often

one of them would whimper, and I'd hand them a piece of the home-pulled taffy I had in my pocket. Edward had promised to eat it quietly, so nobody could see. Betsy had not promised anything. She never did.

Neighbors and friends came. I saw Dorothea Dandridge standing with her father. Her petticoat was black silk and draped over a flannel underskirt. It made almost as much noise as the wind. I saw her smile at John, and his look returned. It was a look I'd never seen on John's face before. And I thought, you can't return something unless it was first given to you.

Grandma fed everyone afterward and hugged us children and rubbed our hands. She was brisk and businesslike and cheerful. She'd seen too much death on the frontier.

After everyone had eaten, Pa, Patsy, and MyJohn went home. We children stayed. And when we arrived home the next day, there was a giant bonfire in the yard.

"What is it for?" Will asked.

Pegg looked at us. "These are your mama's things."

I stood, horror-struck. "What things?"

"Everythin'," Pegg said. "Your pa, he want nothin' from your mama left."

I stood watching the leaping flames against the gold and red sunset of the sky, with bits and pieces of paper or ash in them. And I heard the crackling, and thought, I hope the wind takes the smoke to heaven, where Mama is. Then I ran into the house. Down through the hall to Mama's old room, which was now Patsy and MyJohn's.

It was stripped of curtains, bed hangings, rugs, everything that had belonged to my mother. Patsy stood folding some old fabric that had been imported from England.

"What are you doing?" I demanded.

"Pa wants everything of Mama's burned."

"But to what end?"

"Because he can't bear to look at her things! When you grow up someday and love someone, you'll understand, Anne."

"But mayhap I want to keep something of Mama's."

"Well, you can't. Everything is gone."

On a small side table I spotted a brooch and some hair combs. My eyes sought them out, then met Patsy's.

"They're mine," she said.

"By what right?"

"By Pa's."

"It isn't fair!"

"I'm the oldest, Anne. I remember Mama longer than any of you. As the oldest daughter, Pa said I get to pick what I want. It's due me. And don't you go running to Pa. He's sore grieving."

I ran to her and snatched out of her hands the fabric from England.

"Come back here with that!"

I ran down the hall and bumped into MyJohn. "Here, where are you going? What's wrong?" He held me gently.

"Let me go!" I pounded on him. But he wouldn't.

Skirts raised to keep from tripping, Patsy came upon us and retrieved the fabric.

"It's mine!" I kicked at her then and hit her.

"You do inherit Mama's bad blood!" she shouted at me. "If you're not careful, I'll put *you* in the cellar."

"What is this?"

Pa came out of another room down the hall, which he now slept in. We stood quiet, all of us.

He came toward us, quiet and dignified. "We have just buried your mother. Can't we have some respect for the dead?"

"I was going to burn the fabric, Pa," Patsy said, "and she took it from me. It was Mama's. You wanted everything burned."

Pa held out his hand. Patsy gave him the folded fabric. It was of good cotton, cream-colored, with small red and blue flowers. He stroked it softly. "She held off making a dress of this because it was from England," he said. "She wanted to have a new dress for after Edward was born. She held this fabric, and measured it and draped it, this way and that."

Nobody said anything.

"You may have it, Anne," he said. And he handed the fabric to me.

"Pa!" Patsy started to protest, but his look silenced her.

I held close the fabric that Mama had held and measured and draped. "Thank you, Pa," I said.

Then Pa looked at MyJohn. "I want that room downstairs stripped clean and sealed up."

"Yes sir. I'll see to it."

And to Patsy, "And no more mention of anyone being

put there!" he said sternly. "Haven't these children borne enough?"

Patsy's face flamed. And I knew I'd suffer for this the next time Pa went away.

———

HAD PEGG LOOSENED Mama's strait dress and given her the chance to end her own life?

It was a question I dared not dwell upon, and of course Pegg offered nothing in the way of any intelligence about the matter. In the days that followed, she went about her duties as usual. If anything, she stayed away from me, and I from her.

I sensed the truth between us. And the lies.

And I thought, what good to give words to the matter? To even tell anyone?

Negro servants poisoned their masters and mistresses all the time. Had Pegg poisoned Mama?

If so, she could be hanged. Or be burned alive.

But to what end? To bring more anguish to Pa? To make him the center of gossip?

I'll leave Pegg be, I told myself one moment. And then in the next I'd think, no, I'll tell. But tell what? Where is the proof?

When do you keep a secret, and when do you tell a lie?

And who would listen to me if I told? Mama had started going addled by thinking Pegg was about to poison her.

Patsy might put me in another room in the cellar.

So I kept my silence.

———

THOUGH MAMA HAD been in the cellar room for the last four years, her presence was missed in the house.

We walked around, missing the fact that she was no longer under us all the time. I did, and I know the others did, though we spoke not of the matter.

Truth to tell, we scarce spoke to one another at all. We mumbled at table and avoided each other's eyes.

We were inordinately polite to each other, even the little ones. We shared no memories or sense of loss. We each went about our separate ways, afraid that if we opened our mouths, the memories and sorrow, the blames and regrets, would flow out and create a surge of bitterness that would wipe us out of the house, as if the New Found River had overflowed its banks and was full of hurtful debris to wipe us all away.

———

PA LOCKED HIMSELF in his own room in the two weeks following her death. He ate there; he slept there.

We children did not see him.

And then one evening when we were at table, Pa walked into the dining room. And we all stopped eating and stared.

"This distraught old man must soon be off to Richmond," he said.

MyJohn was the first to unfreeze himself. He got up to pull the chair out for him. Pegg ran to get a plate of food.

"Are you up to it, Pa?" Patsy asked.

"I must be. The convention is going to address questions of public security."

"Why Richmond?" John asked. "It's just a little trading village."

"So as to be out of the reach of Lord Dunmore," Pa said, "who has a force of marines on several warships anchored in the James River, a few miles from Williamsburg."

"Trouble, Pa?" Patsy asked.

Pa took a drink of wine that MyJohn poured for him. "If Dunmore decides to move against our convention and seize its leaders, we'll at least have some warning in Richmond, and a chance to escape. Rather than be trapped in Williamsburg and shipped to England to be drawn and quartered on Tyburn Hill."

"Oh, Pa!" Patsy moaned.

"I'll be back," he said.

And we started talking then about troubles outside the house. It seemed, I thought, as if everyone was grateful to have something to talk about.

———

TWO DAYS LATER Pa rode off for a little town where Shockoe's Creek spilled into the river.

When he left that morning it was snowing again, a March snow, which is always colder, and wetter, and more discouraging than any in midwinter.

As we went back to the breakfast table, MyJohn, who'd spent hours with Pa last night, told us of Richmond.

"It has six hundred souls at most. A modest courthouse, some mercantiles, wharves, tobacco warehouses all belonging to Glasgow firms. The houses cling to the bluff."

"Where will they meet?" John asked.

"St. John's Church, I believe. They're all going, Richard Lee, Peyton Randolph, Colonel Washington, Richard Bland."

"It's important, isn't it?" Will asked.

MyJohn knew more than he was saying. He did not want to frighten us. "Yes," he said, "it is. And I know you all need your pa here right now. Times have been bad. And they are going to get worse before they get better. But I want you to feel you can come to me with anything that troubles you."

He looked across the table at me as he said it.

———

PA CAME HOME in a little less than two weeks. But we'd already read all about his speech in the *Gazette*.

How proud Clementina would have been of Pa, I thought while Patsy stood there in the parlor and read it, her voice rising and falling, as if she were giving a dramatic presentation.

"Oh, oh, listen," she said. "All of you listen to Pa's words!"

So we listened.

I closed my eyes as Patsy read. I thought of Mama, and heard only bits and pieces.

"'It is natural for a man to indulge in the illusions of hope. We are apt to shut our eyes against a painful truth.'"

A painful truth.

"'I am willing to know the whole truth; to know the worst and to provide for it.'"

To know the worst.

"'Let us not, I beseech you, sir, deceive ourselves longer. We have done everything that could be done to avert the storm.'"

We even put her in the cellar for four years.

"'In vain, may we indulge the fond hope of peace and reconciliation. There is no longer any room for hope.'"

Oh, Pa, I thought.

"'They tell us, sir, that we are weak—unable to cope with so formidable an adversary. But when shall we be stronger? Will it be next year?'"

We may never be stronger, Pa.

"'Gentlemen may cry, Peace, peace!—but there is no peace.'"

You know, Pa, more than anybody.

"'Is life so dear, or peace so sweet, as to be purchased at the price of chains and slavery?'"

Or a strait dress?

"'Forbid it, Almighty God. I know not what course others may take; but as for me, give me liberty or give me death!'"

Oh, Patrick, please, give me my freedom or let me die!

———

PATSY FINISHED reading. We all stood dumbstruck. I more than the others. "People are already saying he is the greatest speaker since Demosthenes," she said.

I wanted to tell her it was Mama who had uttered those words about freedom or dying. Not Demosthenes.

I didn't even know who he was. I didn't want to know. Some silly old Greek, likely. She put much store in silly old Greek writings.

I just turned, wiped the tears from my eyes, and ran from the room.

Chapter Twenty-one

APRIL 1775

MY PA IS A HERO now to everybody. After he got back from Richmond, people of all persuasions came to see him. And the traveler's room was always ready with food and drink on the sideboard, a fire glowing, and more bearskin rugs on the floor.

The talk from the room went on long into the night. And much of it had to do with the war that was coming.

Pa was sure it was coming.

Hadn't he insisted at Richmond that "this colony ought to be put in a posture of defense"?

Grandma sent a package by post.

In it were two tomahawks once used by Aunt Annie's husband, Colonel Christian, on the frontier.

SOMETIMES GRANDMA sent packages. Most of the time they contained a new chemise or petticoat for one of us girls, sometimes a new hunting shirt for Pa or the boys.

"A tomahawk," MyJohn said. "I haven't seen a tomahawk around here in ages."

With the package came a letter. "Did you hear what a Tory merchant in Norfolk is saying of your pa? That he never heard anything more infamously insolent than P. Henry's speech!"

Insolent. Give me liberty or give me death.

Patrick, please, give me my freedom or let me die.

"You know," Grandma's letter went on, "those words 'peace, peace,' that your pa cried out in his speech, are in the text from Jeremiah. And I dragged your pa often to hear Mr. Whitefield's sermons when he was a boy. Glad to see they took seed."

So then, I thought, if Pa got "peace, peace" from Jeremiah, isn't it possible he got "liberty or death" from Mama?

I don't know what gave me the notion to put the question to Patsy. But I did, finally. And she got into a regular tempest. "It's Pa's speech! He got it from no one but himself!"

And it was then that she told me that if I mentioned the matter again, she would put me out of the house.

———

I WAS NOT ANGRY with Pa for using Mama's words. I told Pegg about it, and she said that if a person comes on in their life to doing a great thing, the greatness doesn't come from the moment.

"It comes from all the pain they've ever known," she said. "And don't want to know again. It comes from all the times they hurt others, and did no-account things, and couldn't make them right again. And," she said, "it comes from everything they have ever suffered, or given, or become, or been part of."

So I suppose that put Pa in line to do great things.

I was put out with Patsy for not believing Mama had said the words, is all. I felt Mama should have been given at least as much credit as Jeremiah.

———

BUT I DID NOT have time to be in a pet. There were other things I had to worry about.

Betsy, for one. She looked like she'd been living inside a cave these days. After Mama died, I determined to take more care of her.

It was not a simple matter. Betsy was not accustomed to care. She had become used to Patsy's sharp orders, to keeping her fingers busy stitching, to being satisfied to be left alone in a corner with a book and taken no notice of.

She had come to like it that way.

So I made overtures to Betsy.

I taught her how to blow soap bubbles. Would you believe that a child of six had never blown soap bubbles? What had happened here? I wondered. How did Betsy go from being a laughing two-year-old always running free to somebody who looked like they lived in a cave, hiding with a book in a corner?

Will always liked to use a pipe stem for bubble blowing, but I found a quill better for making the bubbles larger.

I taught Betsy how to play Old Man in His Castle. We helped Pegg's husband, Shagg, make building blocks for Edward, and painted them with numbers and letters.

I got her smiling. Not much. Her wan little face offered a crooked, polite smile. And it made me want to cry. But I had to be happy with it, seeing it was all I was going to get.

And then there was John to be worried about, too.

Oh, John looked robust enough. No cave look for him. His shoulders had gotten even broader, and he was looking more and more like Pa these days.

But he was going three times a week now to muster. I watched him at the table when he didn't know I was watching. I saw that his sureness of self was growing as broad as his shoulders. Was it the musters with the militia? Or was it his plans of running Doormouse in the steeplechase this summer?

Or was it Dorothea?

She'd ridden over one day after Pa had come home from Richmond. On her sleek horse and wearing her velvet riding outfit. She'd come for coffee. On her head was a little silk hat with a feather that I knew did not come from hereabouts. It had England written all over it. And she wore delicate leather gloves. Oh, how I envied her pert nose, her gleaming white teeth, her curls, her slim waist!

"Mr. Henry," she said to Pa. "I'm hoping for your son's horse in the steeplechase this summer."

"We're all hoping," Pa said.

"Dr. William Flood's chestnut is running again, I hear.

So is Colonel Taylor's filly. Is it true that this summer the race will be held across the river in Surrey, at Devil's Field? And people will come from both sides of the James?"

"It's true," John said.

"It's a large purse," she said. "I hope your horse wins." Like it was Pa's horse and not John's.

And she was not looking at John. But at Pa.

"I have a surprise for you, Mr. Henry," she said as we were leaving the dinner table. "May I use your pianoforte?"

We all gathered in the parlor. John stood next to the pianoforte as Dorothea sat and smiled sweetly at Pa.

"Did you know they are putting the words of your speech into song?"

Pa shook his head no.

"Well, I was at a gathering in town three days ago, and it is certainly so. Here, let me play and sing it for you."

And she did. *Each free-born Briton's song should be, Or give me death or liberty."*

And I thought, what can I do about John? He already knows how to blow bubbles and play Old Man in His Castle. But what if he went to war? And I can't talk to him every day to see how he is faring? What if I can't watch him?

CLEARLY, THE MENFOLK in our house were expecting war. It was all they talked about.

And they had enough to talk about.

Governor Dunmore issued a proclamation forbidding the appointments of any delegates to the next Congress in Philadelphia.

All gunpowder shipments from England were put to a halt.

Express riders raced through our green, spring countryside, wild of eye, with the news.

"They talk to make themselves brave," Pegg said.

It took a grievous amount of talk between Pa and MyJohn, John and Will, to get brave.

It took polishing of muskets, and making of musket balls. It took the readying of haversacks and shot pouches. And considerable handling of those tomahawks Grandma had sent.

But what they were readying for, I did not know. Nobody did.

And then, of a sudden, it came. The pounding on the door in the middle of the night of April 20. The instant lighting of lanterns.

I stumbled into the hall to see Pa, in black cloth breeches and nightshirt, talking to a messenger at the front door. Then the man left.

"What's happened?" asked MyJohn.

"An armed schooner came to Williamsburg from Burwell's Ferry and took all the powder out of the magazine," Pa said.

"What are you going to do?" John asked.

"Dunmore gave the excuse of slave uprisings. At least four in surrounding counties. Says it is not wise to leave the powder in the hands of agitated people."

I saw MyJohn and Pa exchange looks. Like they knew something the rest of us didn't.

"Whether there are uprisings or not, the powder belongs to the people, not to the government," Pa said.

It was enough. We all knew that now there would be trouble.

Pa insisted we all go about our regular business. For two days he went quietly about the house, studying papers he'd brought home from Richmond, reading his law briefs, riding out to see the spring fields, meeting with men callers in the traveler's room.

Then, on the third night after the governor seized the gunpowder, Pa and the boys left to join the Hanover Volunteers.

The citizens were assembling on the town green in Williamsburg, armed and fearful. And the governor was threatening to free the Negroes.

———

IN THE WEEK that followed, we found out about the war starting up north at Lexington and Concord.

Their war had started before ours. And we had Pa, speechifying.

The week after that, Patsy became terrified. Not of the war. Of our Negroes.

She refused to eat anything until Pegg tasted it first. "They're going to poison us," she said.

Betsy started to cry. Patsy scolded her and, for lack of anything better to call her, said she was a sissy boots. Edward, who was four now and said everything, told Patsy he wanted his morning hominy.

"Pegg has to taste it first," she said. "Wait."

"Want it now!" Edward banged a pewter spoon on the table.

Edward was the darling of the household, and he knew it. He was a cunning child, with his straw-blond hair, his peach-white skin, his smiling blue eyes, and his delicate ears that added to his fairy-child-like appearance.

Patsy slapped his hand, then pulled him off the chair and slapped his bottom. "No breakfast for you."

Edward commenced to wail.

"Don't hit him!" Will scolded. Will was taller than Patsy already, well onto becoming a young man and commissioned by Pa to be head of the household with the other men gone. But he was no match for Patsy.

"Hush. I'm head of this family," she snapped.

I got up and took Edward and Betsy by the hands.

"Where are you going?" Patsy demanded.

"To the kitchen. To have breakfast in peace with the children."

"Don't you dare take those children to the kitchen! Pegg will poison them!"

I left the room. So did Will.

"You hear me?" she yelled.

All I heard was her. Sounding like Mama.

─────

I PULLED THE children outside. Spring had been with us for a fortnight, and nobody had paid mind. Trees were in bloom, crops already growing, new lambs and colts in the fields. If I were spring, I thought, and I got myself all gussied up for these people, I'd pack up and leave soon's I got here.

Edward was still sobbing, and I knelt down next to him. "Don't cry," I said. "Pegg will give us breakfast."

He stood wiping his tears. Then he pointed up to the sky. "I want Mama," he said.

I hugged him tightly. His little body responded. And I said, "Edward, I shall always protect you; please don't cry."

It worked. He and Betsy ran toward the kitchen. But I was crying now instead.

———

IN THE DETACHED kitchen, I did not see the cowed figure in the corner at first. I saw only Pegg and the children running to her, she sitting them down at the old wooden table and pouring them bowls of hominy and honey and milk. She set a bowl in front of me, too. I was about to put the first spoonful in my mouth when I heard the whimper.

"I's hungry, Pegg. Why cain't I eat?"

And there, cowering under a blanket in the far corner, I saw a slight Negro girl I did not recognize.

"Who?" I asked Pegg, but she put her finger to her lips and shook her head. "Hush now." But the children had already seen her and turned to stare.

"You all promise not to tell Neely be here?" Pegg knelt down beside Edward and Betsy. "Can't let Patsy know."

Neely! The girl I'd written my letter to the *Gazette* for! The girl who was always running off, whose master beat her.

I wondered where Will had gone, then minded that he was also to take care of John's horses.

I stared at the girl, but she was hidden in a blanket the color of old mushrooms.

"They won't tell," I assured Pegg. "But why is she

here? I spoke to Pa about her master. And he said the burgesses gave Mr. Estave warning."

"Yeah, well, they didn't warn him enough, did they?" She motioned to Neely to get up, and the brown mushroom turned into a comely girl, who stood, shakily.

She had a round, pretty face. Her dress was of good fabric but torn. Her eyes were like lanterns in a storm, the light in them going off and on. She shied from me.

"He beat her ag'in," Pegg said. She sat the girl down at the table and gave her a bowl of hominy.

Neely ate, about starved. She ate quickly, casting an eye around to see who was watching, like a dog who had been mistreated.

"Neely," Pegg told her, "this be the young miss who wrote that letter to the paper to defend you."

Without looking at me, Neely nodded. "Much obliged."

I couldn't stop watching her. But I knew better than anybody what her presence would cause. "You can't stay here," I said. Patsy would have apoplexy. She would think there was a Negro uprising starting here and now.

"I'se takin' her to the Governor's Palace," Pegg said.

"The Governor's Palace?" Of course! She had heard what the governor was threatening. The Negroes had a better intelligence system than we did.

Pegg went about her business. "Tha's where she wanna go. Gonna ask the governor for help."

"He's got his own troubles now."

"The Negroes part of 'em. He say he gonna free the slaves."

I said nothing.

"Tha's why your pa go ridin' out of here so fast, ain't it?"

"He went to get back the gunpowder," I found myself saying. "He went to defend the honor of Virginia."

Dear God! I sounded like Patsy!

In one swift movement, Pegg pulled Neely to her feet, whipped the blanket off her, then ripped the cotton chemise she wore.

"This!" she said angrily. "This be the honor of Virginia!"

And there I saw the whip marks on Neely's back. The girl bowed her head and whimpered.

So did Betsy and Edward. Quickly I gathered them to me. "Don't cry, children," I said. "There, there, don't cry."

I fetched some rock candy from a bowl and gave them each a piece. I settled them by the hearth, where there was a mother cat nursing her kittens. Soon they became distracted and I went back to Pegg.

"I'm sorry," I said. "My pa doesn't countenance such," I told her, "and you know it, Pegg. So don't go blaming Pa."

She helped Neely adjust her clothing, then gathered her things. "I'se takin' her to the Governor's Palace," she said again.

"I won't stop you."

"I'se takin' a horse and gig."

"I said I won't stop you."

Should I? Was I supposed to? How could I? Then I thought about something. "Are you going to get yourself free?" I asked.

"That sister of yours. Think I doan know what she's about? Thinkin' I gonna poison her? Makin' me taste the food afore they eat it? How you think it make me feel?"

"I know how," I said.

"Was me took care of your mama."

Again I said nothing. I never had learned to go up against Pegg.

"That governor give us our freedom, we ready. At least this girl gonna be ready. She not takin' any more beatin's. Lots of Negroes goin' there. He got an armed guard of Negroes round the palace by now."

I felt helpless, stupid, and foolish. For all my studies, my pa being an important man, I felt like a cornstalk in a hailstorm here.

"My Nancy make the meals. Let Patsy think I'se sulkin'."

They went out the door. "Will you be back, Pegg?" I called after her.

"Maybe I will, and maybe I won't," she said. "I'se thinkin' on it."

Chapter Twenty-two

———

I WAITED AND WAITED for Pegg to return. Oh, how I waited.

"Where is your mama?" Patsy asked Nancy at supper.

"She sulkin'," Nancy answered. "She hurt, 'cause you think she gonna poison you all."

Patsy said nothing. And she did not ask Nancy to taste the food first. But Nancy put the soup tureen down, picked up a spoon, and put some soup in her mouth and swallowed. "I got no fancy to die," she said. Then she stepped back and waited.

Patsy served the soup and we ate.

"It's very good, Nancy," Will said. He sounded a lot like Pa.

Nancy remained solemn-faced but nodded to Will. She liked Will, but then everybody did. "I thank you, Mr. Will; an' you wait an' see what I got for dessert."

It was whipped syllabub. As she put it on the table,

Patsy waved her off. "No more tasting, Nancy, thank you."

Later I sneaked out to the kitchen, where Nancy and Jane were cleaning up. "Any word from your mama, Nancy?" I asked.

"Not yet."

"Do you think she'll be back?"

She turned to me. She was big-boned and dignified. It was hard to think we'd once run barefoot across the lawns together. "You want her to come back?"

"Of course I do!"

"So do I." Then she sighed. "But if she don't, I be your friend, Miss Anne. You know that."

We hugged. Years of friendship lay between us, and I was so confused. What if Governor Dunmore did free the slaves? What would we do without our people?

Worse yet, what would Governor Dunmore do with them? Pa was convinced he'd sell them into slavery to the West Indies.

MAMA USED TO TELL us that God has His reasons for everything. I just wish He'd let on to us on occasion is all.

Pegg didn't return until the next day with the horse and gig. I ran to the kitchen, where I knew she'd be checking on Nancy's bread dough, to ask what had happened.

"All those poor Negroes," she said. She sat down heavily at the table.

"Have you eaten?"

"No."

There was a pot of stew bubbling on the hearth. I gave her a bowl and sat down, too. "What poor Negroes?"

"The ones at the palace. They think this war be for them. To set them free. They all around the palace. Waitin'."

"Where is the governor?"

She laughed. "Gone. On the ship *Fowey,* wif his family. He done brought marines into town. An' he got a cannon at the palace entrance. And the mayor out there, beggin' the people not to attack the palace."

"And Neely? If the governor is gone aboard the *Fowey,* where is Neely?"

"Gone to find him in his ship at the York River. The governor hear that your pa be headed for Williamsburg, wif an army. Tha's why he flee."

I didn't know whether to be glad of this news or unhappy.

When I left her, Pegg was leaning over her bowl of soup. "Never did see nuthin' like the way that girl wanna be free," she was saying. "Never did see nuthin' like it."

———

TWO DAYS LATER I found Pegg alone in the kitchen, crying.

Pegg never cried. She was chopping vegetables and stopping every so often to wipe her face with her apron.

"Pegg?" I asked.

She turned and offered me a weak smile. "Neely dead."

"Dead?"

She went on chopping. "She get herself caught and sent back to her master. He give her eighty lashes."

"Eighty!" Never had I heard such a thing. I went weak.

"Tha's not all. After, he pour hot embers on her back."

I had to sit down. I could not conjure it in my mind. Who did such things? There were no words in me. That frail girl, who just two days ago had been here in our kitchen, eating our food. What manner of people were we?

Still Pegg chopped. "Never did I see a girl who wanted her freedom so bad," she said.

How do they stay sane, I wondered. My own mama went mad for a thimbleful of troubles. Are they stronger than us in their heads?

I put my hand on her shoulder. I hugged her. We cried together. And the only words I could think of were, "I'm going to tell Pa when he comes home."

———

WHEN PA AND THE BOYS came home on the eighth of May, the first thing that caught my attention was how agitated John was.

"They wouldn't let us fight." He took a cup of brandy in the traveler's room. The windows and door were open to the May evening, which was like the silk we weren't allowed to import anymore. You could wrap yourself in it.

But John's mood was as rough as the fabric of his hunting shirt that was hung with fringe about the shoulders and had LIBERTY OR DEATH painted on the back.

"We camped fifteen miles from town," he told us. "A thousand of us. The Tories called us 'shirt men.' And old

Peyton Randolph wouldn't let us attack. So we were discharged."

"Only after Thomas Nelson underwrote the money they offered," MyJohn reminded him. "Dunmore threatened to shell Yorktown from his warship if we came to Williamsburg."

"We've accomplished what we set out to, son," Pa said quietly. "We must act within the bounds of delegated authority."

"Like the militia up in Massachusetts?" John flung at him.

Pa smiled. "The fighting up north requires that we meet again before we battle. At the convention in Philadelphia. And I'm a delegate to the convention."

"Meet," John grumbled. "That's all we do is meet."

"Because we are an organized citizenry," Pa said. "And not a rabble. Come now, let's go to supper."

———

JOHN EXCUSED himself from the table before supper was over and went to the barn.

He was up to something. I knew my brother. As soon as I could do so without making a problem of it, I went to find him.

———

I CAME UPON HIM and Dorothea. In one of the empty stalls.

They were kissing.

I don't know why it looked wrong to me. Certainly

not for the reasons that would be given to any young woman of the day, but for another reason.

I did not trust Dorothea.

Hadn't John seen the way she had cozied up to Pa the last time she came to our house for supper?

She was giggling. John had his arms around her, tight. I left.

———

THAT NIGHT I told Pa about Neely. He was in the front parlor, getting his books and papers ready for the Congress in Philadelphia. A large group of Hanover Volunteers were coming to Scotchtown to escort him on the first leg of the journey, the day after tomorrow.

"Pa."

"Yes, Anne, come in."

"Pa, I must needs speak to you."

He gestured I should sit, and I did. "Pa, Mr. Estave killed Neely, Pegg's niece. He whipped her, then poured hot embers on her back."

"I know, Anne," he said sadly. "I heard."

"She was here, Pa. A couple of days ago."

"Here?"

"Yes, because Pegg is her aunt. Pegg took her to the Governor's Palace for safety, but he was gone. Then she went to find his ship and they caught her. Oh, Pa, I met her! She was so sweet. And scared! How could he do such?"

He held me and I cried.

"We have sent a delegation to his place to bring him to justice, child."

"What justice?" I pulled away from him. "They'll tell him they don't countenance such, and he'll say he's sorry. And Neely is *dead*, Pa!"

He wiped my eyes. "He shall be subject to whatever the courts decide. I promise you."

"And they'll decide nothing."

"Most crimes committed against slaves go unpunished," he admitted, "but whites are betimes tried, convicted, and punished. Still, laws against cruelty to slaves are easy to evade, Anne, which is why he got away with it the last time."

"Pa, you must do something!"

"I'll do everything I can, child. Our servants should have the strongest claim on our charity. They should be well fed, well clothed, nursed in sickness, and never be unjustly treated. I have stood for that, Anne, but to our shame, others don't. And now we're fighting a war and must become free ourselves, first. But I am sure men will bring up slavery, in Philadelphia, at the Congress."

"Talk," I mumbled, "more talk."

"We are civilized men, Anne. We must keep within the boundaries of the law. It's one reason I held back from attacking Dunmore at Williamsburg."

"Estave isn't civilized."

"No, but likely he was acting under the fever of the moment. That's what war does to people, Anne. In some it brings out the latent evil in their nature, and they use it in the name of patriotism. You're a good girl to grieve. We must never close our door to the suffering of humanity. And as soon as I can, I shall visit Neely's family."

"Pa, there's something else."

"Yes, child."

"There's John," I blurted, surprising even myself. It had been in the back of my mind all along.

"Yes. He's young and spirited up. And angry. I know that, too."

"You can't let him go to war when the time comes, Pa."

"When the time comes, he'll have to obey his commanding officer. Don't worry, child."

"Pa, don't let him go, please."

"You have an urgency about you, Anne. Is there a reason?"

"I worry for him."

"I know you do. As do we all worry for him and MyJohn, and all the good men who will make the sacrifice and go. But what I said in my speech, Anne, 'is life so dear or peace so sweet as to be purchased at the price of chains and slavery?'"

"Pa."

"You do John an injustice by not crediting him with more courage. Unless there is something here that I don't know. I haven't been home that much. My children have fair grown up without me. My dog, Charger, scarce recognized me. Tonight he barked when I rode up. Is there something I don't know, Anne?"

When do you tell the truth and when do you lie?

When do you keep a secret? Do you keep it, even if, when it comes out, it will hurt the person, anyway?

I said nothing.

Not even to Patrick Henry, who held sway over learned men. And made them declare for independence and march to war. Who had driven Lord Dunmore onto his ship.

Two days later, Pa left for Philadelphia.

Chapter Twenty-three

OCTOBER 9, 1777

W HEN I AWOKE, it did not come to me for a minute. I lay in my bed, looking around. And then I felt a sense of dread. There was something terrible I had to do this day. For a moment I could not recollect what it was.

And then it came to me.

I must write to my brother John, who was away with the army in New York, and tell him.

Tell him that yesterday Pa had taken to him a new wife, in St. Martin's Church here in Hanover Township.

Pa had wed Dorothea. Some of the wedding guests were still about the house, sleeping downstairs, upstairs, even on the floor in the parlor. And I had to tell John.

———

PA WAS GOVERNOR now. Many was the time I made the trip with Dorothea to the Governor's Mansion in

Williamsburg to see to the decorating, which was not finished yet. Pa still made the trip on horseback to meet with the governor's council and do his work.

The mansion had to be redone before we moved in.

"You can't have animal skins on the floor of the Governor's Mansion, Mr. Henry," Dorothea would say to Pa.

And "We must get those weapons out of the entry hall. They symbolize the Crown's power."

And "I think blue for the draperies in the upstairs chambers. I love blue. Patrick, you must receive visitors and transact business in the middle room upstairs."

Pa was the first governor in the colonies who wasn't appointed by royal authority. And when the mansion was finished, we'd all live there. Not Patsy and MyJohn, no. That was the only good thing about moving. I'd miss MyJohn, but Patsy would no longer be in charge.

I sensed that Dorothea would not be that easy to manage, but she'd be better than Patsy, anyway.

I got up and got dressed. I would go out for a ride on Small Hope this morning, before the rest of the house was up. I often helped Barley exercise John's horses, and the ride would help me think.

What would it be like in the Governor's Mansion? I already knew there were servants and soldiers all over the place. That by eight in the morning there were people already sitting in the parlor off the entrance hall, waiting to see Pa.

Betsy and Edward, now eight and six, loved it. When we went with Dorothea before the wedding, they ran through the sixty-three-acre park, played in Governor

Dunmore's elegant carriage that was still in the carriage house, ran through the ballroom, and hopped about the formal gardens. Betsy almost seemed happy again with the excitement of it.

I dressed warmly and quickly. Outside, the sun was just a promise in the east. Yesterday had been warm, and all the windows in our house had been open when Pa and Dorothea received their guests after the wedding ceremony.

But last evening it turned cold. I put my boots on and went out into the hall to creep out to the kitchen. Pegg would be up, starting breakfast.

"Where are you going?" It was a whisper from the end of the hall. I turned.

Dorothea stood there, wrapped in a shawl, her beautiful hair around her shoulders.

I smiled. "Out for a ride. I often ride early in the morning."

She did not try to stop me, as Patsy would. "Tell Cook, if you see her, that I wish to have hominy cakes as well as eggs and ham for breakfast."

"Yes," I said. She was near in age to Patsy, who was twenty-two.

I went out the back door to the walkway to the kitchen.

"You can no longer appear in plain dress, Mr. Henry," she had told Pa. "You must have black breeches and coat, a scarlet cloak, and a dressed wig. The people will not want the governor of a republican state to be less honored than that of a royal colony."

Pa listened to her. About everything. He was tolerable smitten. And there was nothing any of us could do about it.

———

WHEN DO YOU TELL a secret, and when do you keep a lie?

We did not tell Pa, when Dorothea first started coming regularly to supper at Scotchtown, that John and Dorothea were in love.

"It is Dorothea's place," Patsy whispered to me. "And only she knows what matters lie between her and our brother. If any."

I argued, of course, for John. But it was as if Dorothea had never known him, once she and Pa started walking out. And she was not about to talk of John.

And, thanks to all of us keeping John's secret, Pa never knew of it. That must be noted in Pa's favor.

Then, once there was talk of making Pa governor, after he resigned his command in the army in February of '76, Dorothea was seized with a passion to help him redecorate the Governor's Mansion.

And she was always around Scotchtown, it seemed. Always there were fabrics, bought from Williamsburg shops, on our dining room table. And papers with plans and measurements drawn upon them.

When Pa was sworn in as governor in July of that year, right after the Declaration of Independence was signed, we were all there to see him handed the big key to the mansion. To see him open the front door and walk in and up the great staircase to sit in the middle room at Dunmore's desk.

All but MyJohn and John, who were away at war. All but Will, who was away at college.

We knew the wedding was coming. But there was nothing we could do to stop it. And the reason we didn't tell John until afterward is my fault, too, not only Patsy's.

Patsy wanted Pa to wed Dorothea. "Why, her grandfather was Governor Alexander Spotswood, the best of colonial governors," she told me. "And Mrs. Washington herself is a niece of Dorothea's father. You know Pa will wed again, Anne. It might as well be to someone of gentility, who makes him happy."

"Then write and tell John," I begged.

"Why? He's so far away from home. What can he do?"

"He should know," I insisted.

But she would not. And she forbade me to. I should have, I know. But in this instance, I was glad of Patsy's forbidding me.

In this instance, I made the worst mistake of my life.

Then, somehow, Dorothea was taken with an attack of conscience. And right before the wedding, she told Pa about John. And Pa called me into the parlor at Scotchtown and asked me himself.

———

DOROTHEA WAS THERE. Oh, how I hated that she should be there when Pa and I were to talk. But she was. And she wasn't about to absent herself, either.

"Anne, did you know that John is enamored of Dorothea?" Pa asked me.

I said yes.

"Why didn't you tell me?"

I did not answer.

"Anne, I would not have John's sensibilities hurt. I would have told him early on that Dorothea and I had become close in his absence."

Why didn't Dorothea tell you? I wanted to ask. But I did not. "I don't know, Pa," I said. "John wanted us to keep it a secret."

"According to Dorothea, there was no secret to keep, Anne. Though she fears John might think so. She was never serious about him. I fear she was playing, as she played with so many other beaus." And he smiled at her. "But we ought to write and tell him of our wedding."

" 'We'?" My voice cracked.

Dorothea smiled at me. "It occurred to me that you were closest to him, Anne. Why don't you write to him and tell him of our wedding?"

"Me?" I asked again.

"I shall write, also," Pa said. "But a letter from you would serve him well. And you must back me up, Anne, when I tell him you never told me."

It was agreed then. I would write the day after the wedding. Which was today. Pa would write, too. This very day.

But first I would go to the kitchen to see Pegg.

———

I WALKED OUTSIDE a bit first. Sun rose in the east, streaking the sky with its rosy promise. I knew I was wrong, keeping all those secrets.

So many secrets.

John's love for Dorothea, kept from Pa. Pa's courting her, kept from John.

Mama's saying, "Oh, Patrick, give me my freedom or let me die."

Even riding Small Hope, and dressing as a boy that day, so long ago now, to bring Doormouse home.

Lying to Betsy and Edward about Mama having brain fever.

Keeping Patsy's lies about drinking tea, too long.

Keeping Nancy's lie to Patsy, when she told her Pegg was in the quarters sulking, when indeed her mama was taking Neely to the Governor's Palace for safety. Who knows, but Neely might still be alive today if I'd gone into the house that day and sought help for her.

Lying to Pa when he asked me if I knew of any reason why John should not go to war.

And worst of all, lying to all of them about who would inherit Mama's bad blood.

But every time, I told myself as I walked around the house, every time I thought I was helping the person I was lying for.

And every time I thought I was keeping a secret to protect someone.

And now, this very day, all my lies had come home to roost.

———

OH, IT DID MY HEART good to see the outline of that solid house against the morning sky. To see the trees around it all dressed in red and gold, the smoke coming out of its chimneys, the even lines of white fencing, the horses and cows in the fields.

And I thought, this place of all on earth owns me. And cherishes me. And at the same time is the seat of all my sorrows. And yet it has talons that reach out and grab me, then embrace me.

This place will always be home.

Pegg was in the kitchen, and she knew why I'd sought her out. It must have been written all over me.

"What gonna happen now?" she asked.

I sat at the table, drinking coffee. She was making me some ham and eggs. Fresh biscuits were in the brick oven. The smell near drove me mad.

"We could use you at the mansion, Pegg. Dorothea says the cook can't make biscuits like you."

She set my plate in front of me. "You gonna write to that boy?"

"Yes. Today. Me and Pa both."

She grunted. "Tha's no kinda letter a boy needs when he goin' into battle."

"He's going into battle?"

"Tha's what he wrote to Barley."

"Then, maybe I shouldn't write now."

"You gots to. Your Pa will. And John needs to hear from you."

"I'm not sure, Pegg, how he'll receive the news," I said.

"He take it. He's a strong, good boy."

"No," I said.

She looked at me.

It was time. Time to tell somebody, I decided. If only for the good of my own soul. And she was waiting.

"I never told anybody, Pegg, but I lied about who is going to inherit Mama's bad blood. It's not me. It's John."

Her brown yellow eyes almost seared me with pain, like fire. "Never thought it was you. Knew you were lyin' to protect somebody. You mean to say tha's what your mama tol' you? John?"

"Yes."

"I thought it was a woman's sickness."

"So does everybody in my family. That's why I got away with the lie so long, Pegg. That's why they all believed me."

"But why you *do* this? Why you put the burden on yourself? All these years, takin' Patsy's bad mouth, her orders, her slaps. Never bein' 'lowed to do this or that. Why you didn't say the truth?"

I shrugged. "Because I love my brother, Pegg. Because I knew he would have done the same for me. And because he couldn't have stood what Patsy would have done to him. She would have brought him to insanity. And he isn't a bit addled now, is he?"

"But *why*?" Still she could not understand. "Why not say, if'n you gonna lie, that it be Patsy?"

"Because then she wouldn't have wed MyJohn. We needed MyJohn around here. And he loved her so. And after they wed, I still felt the need to protect John."

"Lord," she breathed. "Lord spare us. And now you gots to write and tell him that his daddy wed the lady he love."

I said nothing.

"Now what?"

"I'm hoping that he's strong enough to abide it, Pegg. I'm hoping that's what I helped him be, all these years."

"An' if he ain't?"

"I can't think on that now. Oh, Pegg, I'm a liar. It's what I am. It's what I do," I wailed.

She got up and put her arms around me while I cried.

"It's what you had to be to make it, chil'. It's what everybody in that house do. An' you had to do it, too, or you never make it."

Chapter Twenty-four

MARCH 1778

WHEN I GOT HOME from my ride that day, nobody scolded because I had missed breakfast.

Pa had received news that British General John Burgoyne was coming through a hundred miles of howling wilderness to attack America from Canada.

I don't know if he got to write the letter that day to John. But I wrote mine.

I told of the wedding, of how we'd soon be living in the Governor's Mansion. How I hated it already. I spoke little of the wedding, however. I did say I was sorry, and that Pa had never known he, John, was taken with Dorothea.

"I think her spoiled and deceitful for not having told him sooner herself, John," I wrote. "And being such, you should be glad to be rid of her."

I told him about his horses and how well they were doing. And how they'd be ready to be raced when he came home again.

IT TOOK ME AWHILE to ponder the why of it. I suppose my letter got there before Pa's. So that by the time Pa untangled himself from worrying about Saratoga and wrote his, John never opened Pa's letter.

We never found out until months later that John did not open it, until it was returned to Pa from General Washington.

With a note from the general himself.

> Although I was not at Saratoga, I have been informed that your son, artillery Captain John Henry, distinguished himself there on the battlefield with great valor. However, after the battle, which was such a victory for us, was finished, young Captain Henry snapped his sword to pieces, flung it to the ground and went raving mad, according to reports, as he walked amongst the American dead and dying, lingering long over the bodies of those he had known so well.
>
> The boy's ill state of health ever since obliged him to quit the service about three months past. I therefore extend to you my sincere concern and best wishes and return to you his letter.

PA SENT BARLEY with money and clothing to bring John home. John was then in New Jersey.

IT WAS CLEAR to me. My letter had gotten to him. By the time Pa's came, he knew everything. So he crumbled it up and put it in his pocket and went to war.

The war I could have kept him from, if I had told Pa the truth about him. Instead of keeping it to myself.

As I'd kept to myself the secret Mama had told me. That he was the one to inherit the sickness of the mind.

I did it to protect John. Now I wonder if not telling made things worse for him.

When do you keep a secret and when do you tell a lie? When do you go too far to protect those you love? When is lying to keep them safe wrong?

I know now. Leastwise I think I do.

AUTHOR'S NOTE

As many experts on Patrick Henry have said, Henry did not leave a paper trail, like George Washington or Thomas Jefferson, so it is difficult to write about him.

It was difficult, indeed; this is the most difficult book I have ever written. And added to the challenge was the fact that no biographer has really reassessed Patrick Henry with an eye cast to the tolerance and understanding our culture has displayed since the 1970s and 1980s, when "secrets" about the founding fathers were aired and the stilted party line given out about them by historians was put aside. When they were finally regarded as human beings and not icons.

I wrote this novel not to sensationalize or diminish Patrick Henry but to acknowledge that in spite of horrendous troubles on the home front, he carried on his work in the cause of liberty. And to illuminate what his sacrifice of time and commitment to his country cost him. And his family.

After deciding to write it, I determined to write the book more from the standpoint of a family adjusting to the mental illness of a mother than from a view of the history of the period.

The Henry family bore the whole burden of the mental breakdown of its wife and mother, Sarah Shelton Henry, because of the attitude toward "lunatics" at the time. In the eighteenth century there were no facilities for people with depression, no mode of treatment, no medicine, and no understanding.

Today Sarah Henry's problem might be diagnosed as severe postpartum depression, and she would be treated with counseling and the proper prescription drugs. In eighteenth-century Williamsburg, Virginia, the only course for Patrick Henry to follow was to put her in that part of the jail in town reserved for "lunatics," to be chained, bled, blistered, given laudanum—the drug of choice at the time—put in a dunking chair, and confined in a cell that was eleven feet square. And recovery was not an option.

Patrick Henry would not do that. He chose the solution of putting her in the cellar of his own home, where, history tells us, he had a slave woman care for her. And, legend has it, when home, he would go down every day to feed her.

Imagine the anguish of this man! And the confusion and hurtful consequences to his children! I thought the story worth telling, but first I had to imagine it, because all the books written on Patrick Henry focus on his greatness (which I never set out to question) and usually only a paragraph is given to his home problems.

So I imagined it, using all my research. The most I could get about the situation was a report from Dr. Hinde, who was caring for Sarah: "Here at Scotchtown his family resided, whilst Henry had to encounter many mental and personal afflictions known only to his family physician. While this towering master-spirit was arousing a nation to arms, his soul was bowed down and bleeding under the heaviest sorrow and personal distress. His beloved companion had lost her reason and could only be restrained from self-destruction in a strait-dress."

Research tells us that Sarah died in early February of 1775, at the age of thirty-seven, just weeks before Henry gave his immortal cry of "liberty or death."

To flesh out the story, I had to ask myself questions. Why was Sarah in a strait dress? And being thus confined, could she not, before her death, have begged Patrick, "Give me my freedom or let me die"?

Could that heart-wrenching cry have lingered in his soul three weeks after, when he went to St. John's Church in Richmond to the Second Virginia Convention? Could those words have found voice in his passionate liberty-or-death speech?

His own mother, referring to that speech, reminded his family that the words "peace, peace" were in the text of Jeremiah that a young Patrick Henry had heard so often when his mother took him to hear George Whitefield, the famous evangelist preacher. And the Reverend

Samuel Davies, whose sermons she would make Patrick repeat over and over.

Evangelists delivered sermons with power and drama. It is told to us that on the way home from these sermons, in the carriage, young Patrick would stand and try to echo the style of these men.

My point, made by Anne in the novel, is that if Patrick Henry borrowed from Jeremiah, could he not also have borrowed from his own wife? And so it is that historical fiction writers build on facts and take the leap of imagination.

But what is really true in this story and what is imagination-driven?

It is true that Martha Henry (Patsy), as Patrick and Sarah's oldest child, took charge of the younger children once her mother had a mental breakdown. And it is true that John Fontaine, her intended, was her cousin and helped with the children and the plantation management before and after they wed. Indeed, Patsy is cited as "the glue that held the family together," the person who made it possible for Patrick Henry to pursue the business of inspiring the country to freedom.

But what would that mean to the younger children? How many younger sisters can stand being bossed around by an older one? How many older ones could avoid the trap of abusing their authority?

So I added the tension between Anne and Patsy. History tells us that "Anne was plain and outspoken and had a streak of stubbornness." This fit in nicely with the character I was planning for Anne.

As for Sarah Henry's "second sight," that is my invention, although Sarah certainly did have ravings in her madness. The instances of her trying to drown baby Edward and running off with Betsy in a storm only reflect the need to put her in a strait dress.

Many people of the time feared slave uprisings, and those mentioned in the book did happen, as did the terrible flood. So it is entirely possible that Sarah would be fearful that Pegg was out to poison her.

John Fontaine's name, "MyJohn," is my own invention. I wanted this dear man to have an affectionate name, and it cleared up confusion since he had the same name as Patsy's brother.

The character of Neely (I gave her that name) is taken from history. In actuality, this unfortunate girl belonged to Virginia's official vintner, Andrew Estave. And her story is true, right up to her disastrous end.

At the time of the Gunpowder Plot, in 1775, slaves did flee to the Governor's Palace in Williamsburg to take advantage of the freedom promised to them by royal Governor John Murray Dunmore.

From all these facts, I put together my story, allowing my characters to lead me. Patsy, by being afraid to wed because of her mother's sickness, and Anne, by finding out from her mother that John would inherit the madness, and then lying to protect John. And so the web of family secrets, lies, and mistrust grows, as it does in all families where secrets become a way of life.

And so, in her part of the book, Anne's dilemma: "When do you tell the truth and when do you lie? Do you lie to protect someone? Is it wrong to keep a secret, when, if you tell, someone gets hurt?"

This is a common problem for teens. And adults.

Indeed, John did inherit his mother's proclivity for depression. Just as I have portrayed. He went mad right after the Battle of Saratoga, in 1777, when he snapped his sword and wept on the battlefield as he walked amongst the dead. And this was no temporary grief. Within three months, he resigned from the army. And his father had to send a servant to fetch him home.

Some historians assert that John was devastated because his father married Dorothea Dandridge. Is that why he never opened his father's letter? And General Washington returned it to Patrick Henry when he told him of his son's condition? History tells us John was smitten with Dorothea, that she was the age of Patsy, and that Patrick Henry married her not knowing of the connection she had had with his son John. Although all his other children knew of the romance.

So, then all I had to do was connect the dots.

As for Clementina Rind, her role in my book follows fact. She was a powerful force in the community and an independent woman of the times. All the letters from the *Gazette* are real, with the exception of the one written by Anne.

According to all accounts, Patrick Henry was a wonderful father. He allowed his children freedom of movement and thought. In a forty-three-year period, he had seventeen children. As a history buff and lover of our country's past, I chose to bring his first family to life, to make them human, to give them dimension.

Also, I have always wanted to create a book in which something terrible is going on within a household that makes what is going on in the outside world seem mild by comparison. In this novel, I have come as close to that theme as I could.

BIBLIOGRAPHY

PAPERS

News from the Henry Tree, the Patrick Henry Descendants' Branch Newsletter. Brookneal, Va.

Newsletter of the Red Hill Patrick Henry National Memorial. Patrick Henry Memorial Foundation, Brookneal, Va.

BOOKS

Campbell, Norine Dickson. *Patrick Henry: Patriot and Statesman.* Old Greenwich, Conn.: Devin-Adair Company, 1969.

Child, Maria. *The Girl's Own Book.* Old Sturbridge Village: Applewood Books, 1834.

Coffman, Suzanne E. *Official Guide to Colonial Williamsburg.* Williamsburg, Va.: Colonial Williamsburg Foundation, 1998.

────── *Williamsburg—Three Hundred Years Freedom's Journey.* Williamsburg, Va.: Colonial Williamsburg Foundation, 1999.

Holton, Woody. *Forced Founders, Indians, Debtors, Slaves, and The Making of the American Revolution in Virginia.* Published for the Omohundro Institute of Early American History and Culture, Williamsburg, Va. Chapel Hill, N.C.: University of North Carolina Press, 1999.

Kolchin, Peter. *American Slavery, 1619–1877.* New York: Hill and Wang, a division of Farrar, Straus and Giroux, 1993.

Mayer, Henry. *A Son of Thunder: Patrick Henry and the American Republic.* New York: Franklin Watts, 1986.

Meade, Robert Douthat. *Patrick Henry, Patriot in the Making.* Philadelphia and New York: J. B. Lippincott Co., 1957.

Osborne, J. A. *Williamsburg in Colonial Times.* Richmond, Va.: Dietz Press Publishers, 1935.

Williams, George F. *Patrick Henry and His World.* New York: Doubleday and Company, Inc., 1969.

ABOUT THE AUTHOR

ANN RINALDI is an award-winning author best known for bringing history vividly to life. Among her books for Harcourt are *A Break with Charity: A Story about the Salem Witch Trials*, an ALA Best Book for Young Adults and a New York Public Library Book for the Teen Age, and *Hang a Thousand Trees with Ribbons: The Story of Phillis Wheatley*, also a New York Public Library Book for the Teen Age.

A self-made writer, Ms. Rinaldi never attended college but learned her craft through reading and writing. As a columnist for twenty-one years at *The Trentonian* in New Jersey, she learned the art of finding a good story, capturing it in words, and meeting a deadline.

Ms. Rinaldi attributes her interest in history to her son, who enlisted her to take part in historical reenactments up and down the East Coast, where she cooked the food, made the clothing, and learned about the dances, songs, and lifestyles that prevailed in eighteenth-century America.

Ann Rinaldi has two grown children and lives with her husband in central New Jersey.

1. Should Pa have warned Patsy that he suspected her mother's depression? What reasons might justify his not doing so? Is Patsy selfish to worry for her own sanity? What other ways might the family deal with Mama's madness besides imprisoning her in their cellar?

2. Pegg and Patsy negotiate for authority over the children. What are the benefits of Patsy retaining control of the younger kids? Do you think she made the right decision? Why or why not?

3. When Pa postpones Patsy's marriage for a year, is he being hypocritical, or is he a caring father who has learned from his own mistakes? Isn't her role of managing the Henry household during her engagement the very kind of responsibility he fears will send her into depression?

4. Why is Patsy so bossy with Anne? What does MyJohn mean when he says that at Anne's age, hate comes easily? What are some ways that Patsy and Anne could resolve their differences?

5. Pegg says that if a person ends up doing something great, the greatness doesn't come from the moment. What does she mean? Do you agree with her?

6. Anne wonders how Pegg and the other slaves can stay the same in the face of their troubles when her mother, a privileged white owner, couldn't deal with her own troubles. How might you explain why Mama falls into depression while the Henry slaves do not?

7. Is there an answer to Anne's most nagging question: When do you keep a secret and when do you tell? Should Anne reveal the identity of the child who will inherit her mama's madness? Would telling the truth change anything?

8. Pa tells Anne that even though their family is broken, she must enjoy the pieces. He also advises her to look outside the family for her happiness. How can she do both?

Have you read these Great Episodes paperbacks?

SHERRY GARLAND
Indio

KRISTIANA GREGORY
Earthquake at Dawn
Jenny of the Tetons
The Legend of Jimmy Spoon

LEN HILTS
Quanah Parker:
Warrior for Freedom, Ambassador for Peace

DOROTHEA JENSEN
The Riddle of Penncroft Farm

JACKIE FRENCH KOLLER
The Primrose Way

CAROLYN MEYER
Where the Broken Heart Still Beats:
The Story of Cynthia Ann Parker

SEYMOUR REIT
Behind Rebel Lines:
The Incredible Story of Emma Edmonds, Civil War Spy
Guns for General Washington:
A Story of the American Revolution

ROLAND SMITH
The Captain's Dog:
My Journey with the Lewis and Clark Tribe

THEODORE TAYLOR
Air Raid—Pearl Harbor!:
The Story of December 7, 1941